SHOOTER

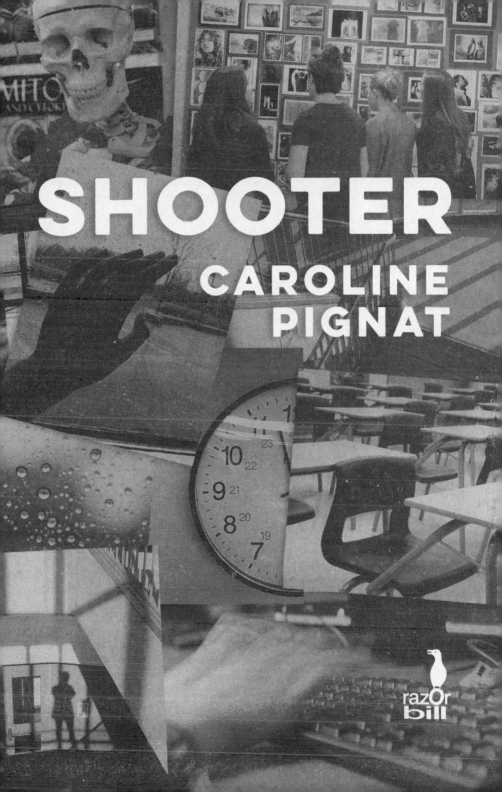

SHOOTER

CAROLINE PIGNAT

razOr
bill

RAZORBILL
an imprint of Penguin Canada Books Inc., a Penguin Random House Company

Published by the Penguin Group
Penguin Canada Books Inc., 320 Front Street West, Suite 1400, Toronto, Ontario M5V 3B6, Canada

Penguin Group (USA) LLC, 375 Hudson Street, New York, New York 10014, U.S.A.
Penguin Books Ltd, 80 Strand, London WC2R 0RL, England
Penguin Ireland, 25 St Stephen's Green, Dublin 2, Ireland (a division of Penguin Books Ltd)
Penguin Group (Australia), 707 Collins Street, Melbourne, Victoria 3008, Australia
(a division of Pearson Australia Group Pty Ltd)
Penguin Books India Pvt Ltd, 11 Community Centre, Panchsheel Park, New Delhi – 110 017, India
Penguin Group (NZ), 67 Apollo Drive, Rosedale, Auckland 0632, New Zealand
(a division of Pearson New Zealand Ltd)
Penguin Books (South Africa) (Pty) Ltd, 24 Sturdee Avenue, Rosebank, Johannesburg 2196, South Africa

Penguin Books Ltd, Registered Offices: 80 Strand, London WC2R 0RL, England

First published in Razorbill hardcover by Penguin Canada Books Inc., 2016

Published in this edition, 2017

1 2 3 4 5 6 7 8 9 10 (RRD)

Cover images: iStock.com/StonRohrer

Text design: Lisa Jager and Erin Cooper
Manufactured in the U.S.A.

Library and Archives Canada Cataloguing in Publication

Pignat, Caroline, author
Shooter / Caroline Pignat.

ISBN 978-0-14-318758-5 (paperback)

I. Title.

PS8631.I4777S56 2017   jC813'.6   C2015-907788-5

eBook ISBN 978-0-14-319694-5

American Library of Congress Cataloging in Publication data available

Visit the Penguin Canada website at **www.penguinrandomhouse.ca**

Penguin
Random
House

For Liam and Marion

We are all pretty bizarre. Some of us are just better at hiding it, that's all.

—ANDY, *THE BREAKFAST CLUB*

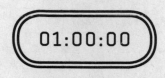
01:00:00

ALICE

"Hey . . . you okay?" The deep voice echoes as I come to, flat on my back on the cold tile. A huge rabbit leans over me.

Yes, rabbit. Whiskers. Buck teeth and ears. Tartan vest—the works. My head aches. I don't have to touch the lump pulsing on my brow to know it's there.

"What happ—?"

"You came barreling in," the rabbit says, but its wide smile never moves. Like it's speaking inside my head. "You tripped and fell."

Down the rabbit hole?

I always dreamed of that as a little girl. That one day I'd find a way into those books I loved. Has it finally happened?

I try to get my bearings as my eyes struggle to focus, but there is no magic beyond the rabbit. Only the white brick wall on which hang three oddly shaped sinks of some kind. My gaze drifts back to the stained ceiling tiles.

Where am I?

The rabbit stands and moves past me. Paper tears. Water runs. I glance over to see it standing at a wide marble semicircular sink.

The washroom?

It's all wrong. And yet, so familiar. Flecked marble sink. Rusted paper-towel holder on the white brick wall. Two beige metal stalls in the far corner. Only everything is mirror opposite, as though I'm in some alternate reality.

One with giant, telepathic rabbits.

Its whiskered, furry face floats above me, going in and out of focus as it kneels beside me again.

My, what short ears you have for a rabbit.

Frowning, I blink a few times.

"You don't look so good," it says.

And that voice—it's all wrong. Everyone knows a rabbit in a tartan vest has a British accent.

"Curiouser . . ." I mumble. The room spins and I groan.

"Here." It presses the wet wad of paper on my forehead and some of the spinning slows.

A large, brown, shaggy paw grips my shoulder. "Do you think you can sit up—?"

"I'm coming in!" a girl's voice calls. "Girl entering the boys' washroom. So, like, stop . . . whatever you're doing."

I half expect to see Mrs. Rabbit come bounding in. Actually, I'm kind of disappointed it's just a girl. In one hand, she clutches a stack of yellow flyers. The other shields her eyes from seeing whatever mysteries of the boys' washroom she'd rather not know. Her hair is straight, long and glossy black. Her red lips, full and almost heart-shaped. Her skin, flawless. She's Asian. A life-sized china doll? But no, she is real enough.

"Isabelle Parks?" The name floats up and out of me.

She uncovers her eyes, shrieking as she takes in the bizarre scene: me, flat on my back beneath this gigantic, looming animal.

"Ohmigod!" Isabelle drops her papers and runs at us. "Get off of her! Get off of her right now, you perv!" She thrusts her knee hard in the animal's side and shoves it over with both hands. Grunting, the rabbit keels over and sprawls with a curse among the yellow flyers scattering across the floor.

"Are you okay?" Isabelle takes my arm and helps me sit.

The room whirls around me like the Mad Tea Party ride. I feel like I'm going to throw up, just like I did ten years ago in that horrible teacup.

"You see it too?" I ask, relieved to know I'm not actually hallucinating. We glance at where the large creature now sits lounging against the far wall, long legs stretched out, huge feet splayed on either side. I eye it suspiciously, half expecting it to disappear in a poof of sparkles. "The rabbit—you can see it, right?"

"What?" Isabelle's dark eyes narrow. She looks at me like I am crazy then goes over to it and kicks the rabbit's foot. "Did you, like, drug her?" she demands. "Is that it, Hogan? Like roofies or something?"

"Ya, Izzy. That's exactly it," the rabbit says. "I have this thing for dressing up like a loser and molesting helpless nerds in the boys' bathroom."

Wait—what? Molesting?!

It raises its furry arms in mock-defeat. "My secret's out. You caught me." Then it shoves its paws up against its puffy cheeks. "Just shut up and help me."

Sighing, Isabelle grabs its face in both hands and cranks hard, ripping head from body in one fierce twist like some kind of psycho vampire killer. The head falls to the floor and rolls to a stop beside me, where it vacantly stares at me with its googleeyes. I don't know whether to scream or laugh or vomit—or maybe all three.

"It's hotter than hell in there." The rabbit's deep voice is coming from its body, still resting against the wall. Headless, yes, but not decapitated, exactly. More like cracked open, like one of

Gran's rosy-cheeked nesting figurines. A doll in a doll in a doll. The furry costume ends at the thick neck and sweaty head of some guy. Some huge guy. He's rubbing his face with his paw, swiping it up his red-faced scowl and over his head as his blond hair juts out in angry spikes. My stomach lurches again—only this time, it's in recognition.

Hogan King. As in, the Hulk.

How did I end up in here with that guy?

The Hulk yanks off his furry mitt and plucks the smoking cigarette left balanced on the edge of the porcelain urinal. Even in a bunny suit and plaid vest he scares me. Anger radiates off of him like distorting heat waves—burning fierce from his cold, blue eyes as they meet mine. I look away.

Did he follow me?

Hit me?

The tremor in my stomach ripples up my back and down to my fingertips as I reach for my forehead.

Did he drag me in here . . . to molest me?

I can't stop shaking. Can't stop imagining the story that might have happened if Isabelle hadn't come in and saved me.

"No smoking." Isabelle points up at the small metal sign.

Is she crazy? Surely she knows better than to rile the Hulk.

He glowers at her, but she only shrugs. "I don't make the rules."

"And I don't follow them." He takes a long drag and blows in our direction. It smells strange. But everything in here has that mystery man-tang. I glance at the filthy floor, the graffitied stall, the stained urinal, the smeared mirror. Some things are better left a mystery.

"Still the badass, Hogan?" Isabelle pulls a slim silver phone from her jean shorts' pocket. She eyes the floor, the stall, and, disgusted, eventually shifts over to lean against the wall. "I don't know why Wilson insisted we use you. You're, like, not even part of Student Council."

The muscles in his jaw clench.

"I mean, seriously." She texts as she talks, like we aren't worth her time or attention. "You've missed every Spirit Club meeting. You're always late to class—when you come. You have, like, zero enthusiasm." She glances up momentarily. "No offense."

It always surprises me how she can do that, add "no offense" to any statement and assume none is taken. Yet not once has anyone, ever, in all our years together at school, once told her, "You're really mean sometimes. No offense."

Isabelle continues, "You quit sports and skip most classes— you basically hate school." She looks up at him once more. "And now you're stoned."

I wave in front of my face and try to stand but stagger into the garbage can and spill trash at Isabelle's feet.

I must be stoned too! Drugged, definitely.

I felt like this before—when I had my wisdom teeth out and Gran had to practically carry me to the truck to go home. No, it's okay, I protested, I can fly, Gran. I can fly! Hand on the wall for stability, I look into the cracked mirror, searching for a portal out of here—but I see only my pale face, the welt, angry and red on my forehead, my pupils wide and black in the blue iris. But, thankfully, they are the same.

No, no concussion at least.

I've had them before. In part because I'm a klutz, in part because of Noah. People who have mild traumatic brain injuries are more susceptible to having another.

Where did I read that? Dr. Schmidt's office, maybe?

It's only when they both look at me that I realize I'm speaking aloud.

"It's okay . . . I'm good," I say awkwardly. "Well, back to normal anyway." Neither speaks. Their expressions clearly tell me they think I am anything but normal. "So . . . yeah." I tuck my hair behind my ear, unsure of what to say next.

Fortunately they just dismiss me and return to their conversation.

The Hulk turns back to Isabelle. "It would take a lot more than a few drags to get me stoned. I just needed some pep before the pep rally." He says it in a girly voice, like the very concept of pep rallies is ludicrous.

"Like I said," Isabelle scoffs, "perfect choice for school mascot."

"We have a mascot?" I blurt. I've attended St. Francis Xavier High School since grade 7, and in the six years I've been here we've never had a mascot—unless you count those weird comic book characters this year, Professor somebody, and that other one with the helmet. But that's just kids messing around. They aren't real mascots. Mind you, neither is this mangy character smoking up on the bathroom floor.

Isabelle glances at me. "See? No one even knew we had one. And I'm, like, every school should have a mascot. So I was going to get us one, something really cool like a Viking. Then Wilson tells me we already have a mascot assigned. A fisher. I'm, like, seriously? A fisher? What brilliant school board official came up with that? Anyway, I figured promoting it, you know, having it lead the cheering at games and pep rallies would be good for school spirit, even if it wasn't as cool as a Viking. The mascot was my idea." She turns back to the Hulk. "He was not."

He shrugs. "Talk to Wilson."

"'Fitting the suit,'" she says, with dramatically mimed air quotations, "does not make you mascot material."

And a mascot who smokes? That's even worse.

The Hulk glares at me and I realize, once again, I've blurted my thoughts. But it's true. Grampa smoked cigarettes his whole life and it cost him. "It really wrecks your cardiovascular system," I add. The Hulk's breathing grows louder and I cringe. "I mean . . . if you're planning on cheering . . . or doing cartwheels . . . and mascot stuff . . ."

Cartwheels? Why in God's name do I keep talking to the Hulk? Even I know the gossip about his suspensions, his arrests—his infamous temper. Rumor is he killed his brother, but that can't be true. They'd never let a murderer loose in a high school. Right? Unless . . . unless it's some kind of high-school-halfway-house thing.

I look back at him to find his eyes drilling into mine. And then it happens.

The babble.

Any time I find myself at the center of unwanted attention, usually thanks to my brother's behavior, I go on autopilot. Other trapped creatures spray ink, quills, or stink as a defense. Apparently, I spew words.

Babble, then bolt. That's my strategy. Only this time, there's nowhere to run.

"Yeah . . . cartwheels," I continue, feeling the panic rise hot around my chest and neck, "or jumping. Because you do kind of look like a rabbit with the floppy ears and all. Still, your ears are a bit short for a rabbit's. Unless you are a short-eared rabbit? Like an American Fuzzy Lop? Or maybe a Mini Lop?"

His scowl darkens.

"But, clearly, you're a fisher. Vicious. Mean. You've got that down. We get fishers on the farm." I fiddle with my fanny pack. "Fun fact: a fisher is one of the few animals that'll eat a porcupine—"

Isabelle raises her eyebrows—but not in that that's-amazing kind of way, more in that are-you-freaking-kidding-me-right-now look. She waits for me to stop. I wish she'd just interrupt me all together.

"—but I don't know why we even call them fun facts, really," I say, "because they're facts, of course, but if you think about it, they're not really—"

"Oh. My. God," she snaps. "Do you, like, ever shut up?"

"—fun." I breathe, glad to finally let someone else take the spotlight.

"Still the bitch, Izzy?" The Hulk exhales a gray halo over his head and smirks. "Some things never change."

HOGAN

Nerd Girl finally shuts up, but she's still swaying a bit as she backs up to the door. "So, uh, I'm gonna go now," she mutters. "I really should get to class . . ."

"What are you talking about?" Izzy looks at her like she's crazy. "Hello? We're in lockdown."

"Lockdown?" Nerd Girl frowns. I guess she hit her head harder than I thought.

"Well, duh." Izzy rolls her eyes and goes back to her texting. "Mr. Wilson just called it, and this was the only unlocked door. Why else would we be in this stinkhole? Maybe you like to hang here, but being stuck in here with you guys is, like, the last place I wanna be. No offense."

"It's just . . ." Nerd Girl is shaking. Her big blue eyes get all watery. She looks at me. At the door. Back at me. "I don't remember . . ."

Izzy stops texting and gives me that look again. Like I did something wrong.

"What?" I snap. Do they seriously think I had something to do with it? "Look." I speak loud and slow so they hear it. So they get it. "I was in here getting this stupid costume on when Wilson announces we're in lockdown. Someone starts banging on the girls' door and next thing she comes flying in here, trips over that," I wave at the red gym bag by the door, "and hits her head on the sink. End. Of. Story."

"So why were you holding her down?" Izzy asks, with that accusing eyebrow raised.

"I was helping her up."

The two of them look at me like I'm speaking bull. Screw it. Screw them. I take a drag.

Exhale. Inhale. Exhale.

Just breathe, like Coach Dufour says. Sometimes even that is hard enough. My chest tightens. It's so freaking hot in this stupid costume.

Inhale. Exhale. Deep. Slow.

Nerd Girl stares at the floor but doesn't sit down. Izzy goes back to her phone. I pick up the fisher head and twist one of the whiskers around my finger. I knew this mascot crap was a stupid idea. I told him. But Wilson called it an "opportunity," a "chance to give back to the school."

Give back? What the hell did St. F-this ever give me?

Like you deserve anything anyways.

And Wilson is all, "It's not too late to redeem yourself." How will jumping around in a fur suit, making a total fool out of myself in front of the whole school, on purpose, do me any good? Why does Wilson even care, anyways? There's no redeeming me. I know that. My teachers know that. They've given up asking why I miss work, miss class, miss detention. I can tell by the way they look at me. The way Dad looks at me. The way Izzy doesn't look at me. They've all given up on me. Why won't Wilson?

Screw it. I'm not doing it. He can expel me if he wants.

The whisker snaps, uncoiling itself from my purpled finger.

Izzy looks over at me and rolls her eyes again. This time, I rip out a whole fistful of whiskers. She just snorts and goes back to texting.

But Nerd Girl can't stop watching me, all wide-eyed and twitchy. She looks away when I catch her staring. Hell, she's even trembling. Yeah. She's afraid of me. Can't stand being near me. Whatever. I get it, though.

I can't stand to be around me either.

We sit for a few minutes, the silence broken by the click-click of Izzy's texting. A sound she could have muted, but no, not Izzy.

"Ughhh," Izzy moans in her overly dramatic way, like she's always on stage. Like we're always her audience. But I can't stop watching. "Why do we even have these drills? Hello? This is Birchtown. The boonies. Geez, it's not like we're living in some inner-city gangland."

"Maybe it's not a drill," Nerd Girl says. "Maybe it's another one of those pranks. It is a Friday."

"I doubt it," Izzy says. "You think those idiots would try pranking a lockdown?"

"Well, idiots aren't typically known for being intelligent," Nerd Girl says. She looks at me and her face goes all red. "Not that you're an idiot . . . I mean . . . statistically speaking . . . uh, jocks and . . . criminals aren't very . . ."

She mumbles on.

Yeah, a lockdown prank sounds exactly like something those guys would do. They've been pulling the fire alarm every Friday for weeks now, setting up their stupid jokes after we evacuate, then painting their red-circled X. It's all over the school, like it's their calling card. Total Marvel rip-off. Some kids even started wearing homemade T-shirts with the X or "Brotherhood of Mutants." Lame. Still, I got to miss a few tests thanks to these X-Men geeks. I glance down at my costume. And maybe even the dumbass pep rally today. But, even I have to admit, a lockdown is taking this prank thing to a whole other level.

"Wilson's not gonna like this." Izzy rolls her eyes. "At that last assembly two weeks ago, he told the whole school that if the pranks didn't stop, our extracurriculars would. Can you believe it?! No dance. No sports. He even threatened to cancel my prom." She shakes her head in frustration. I knew somehow she'd make even this about her. "Why do I have to suffer because some stupid X-morons, whoever they are, get off on playing stupid pranks? It's not my fault . . ." She glances back at her phone, more interested in whatever conversation is going on there.

I don't blame her.

ISABELLE

BRI: Where you at?

Helloooo—earth to Izzy? You back in class?
Getting the evil eye from Carter because your
phone keeps buzzing?

BUZZ!!
BUZZ!!
BUZZ!!
Mwah ha ha ha!

IZZY: Got caught in the stairwell putting up flyers.
You'll never guess where I ended up.
Or with who.

BRI: Library?
Not the psycho janitor's closet?

IZZY: Worse.

BRI: I dunno . . . that closet's pretty creepy.
Lead pipe, in the conservatory, with Colonel Mustard?

IZZY:	Try: Hogan. With a joint. In the boys' bathroom.
BRI:	OMG!!! EWWWWW!!!!!!!! Hands off!
IZZY:	Nice. It was a long time ago. Just one kiss. Do you have to keep bringing it up?
BRI:	:/ I meant the bathroom—that's like ground zero for boy cooties. Seriously. I saw a documentary on that. Don't even touch the walls.
IZZY:	Too late.
BRI:	Ew. Ew. Ew. Go wash your hands.
IZZY:	No thanks. Sink looks like a science experiment.
BRI:	So . . . Hogan? Seriously? Is it just the 2 of you?
IZZY:	No. Another girl. At least I'm not the only one.
BRI:	Who?
IZZY:	I forget her name. That weird guy's sister.
BRI:	?
IZZY:	The one that mops with the janitors in the caf.
BRI:	Noel?
IZZY:	Ya. His sister. Wears those dog T-shirts and that fanny pack.
BRI:	Oh ya. Dresses like a tourist.
IZZY:	Well she's lost for sure.
BRI:	LOL! Lost In the 80s.
IZZY:	Where are you?

BRI:	Main office. Under secretary's desk by the copiers. Wilson can't see me txt here. I was photocopying more flyers when he called lockdown.
IZZY:	Weird time to have a drill.
BRI:	You shoulda seen the secretaries bolt. Single file to the staff room. You'd think it was real.
IZZY:	Probably "hiding" in the staff room cracking open their TGIF wine.
BRI:	So did Darren ask you to prom yet?
IZZY:	No. Why?
BRI:	Just wondering.
IZZY:	Maybe he's taking his time—working on a big promposal. Maybe this drill is it. Dress up like a cop and go door-to-door looking for me. Give me a rose, ask me to prom and charge me with "stealing his heart." *sigh*
BRI:	You think Wilson would let him do that? A lockdown is a big deal.
IZZY:	Hello?! So is my prom. We only get to do this once . . . And it has to be perfect.
BRI:	He would look hot in a uniform. Just saying. ;)
IZZY:	He's taking so long to ask. I worry he's thinking about asking someone else. I know, I'm being stupid.
BRI:	Really?? WHO? Did he say anything?
IZZY:	No. Just a feeling I get sometimes.
BRI:	Who knows, Iz, someone else might sweep you off your feet. Maybe even the Hulk. ;) Throw you over his shoulder. Neanderthal style. Fisher costume—kinda like a uniform.

14

	Might be hot . . .
	. . . and you are such an animal lover. :P
IZZY:	Don't. Even. Go there.
	If Darren doesn't ask, I'm not going.
BRI:	WHAT?! You have to go!! You've been planning it all year.
	The band. The decorations. Your dress! OMG the dress!
IZZY:	Like I wanna show up SOLO at my prom.
	What would everyone think?!
	Not gonna happen. I'd rather stay home.
BRI:	Officer Scott just arrived.
IZZY:	Good. They should start unlocking the rooms soon.
	The sooner this drill is over the better.
BRI:	Hot cop with him, too.
IZZY:	You need help. Seriously.

ALICE

The pounding in my head eventually slows to a pulse in the growing lump. What I need is ice, but for now a cold compress will do. Come to think of it, didn't the Hulk give me one just as Isabelle burst in? Didn't he try to help me up? Maybe he is telling the truth. After all, being a total klutz sounds way more like me than being the desired target of a sexual assault. I stand next to him as I crank the paper towel, rip it off, and move to the opposite side of the sink, as far as possible from where he sits.

He is the Hulk, after all.

The foot pedal squeaks as I press it. A pathetic trickle of water drips onto my wadded paper towel. The Hulk sits on the other side of the marble trough, staring intently at the stall doors across from him, breathing fiercely. Sidelong I watch him, mesmerized by his energy and intensity, the way the muscles in his cheek and jaw clench, how his nostrils flare as he inhales and exhales. He's a mass of angry muscle just looking for a reason to charge, kind of like the bull at our neighbor's farm. Gran always warned me about it, told me to never EVER cross that fence. Yet, here I am inside its very pen.

"I think it's wet enough," he says, not looking at me.

I jump and the sopping paper falls into the filthy basin, but there is no way I'm going near him to get more. I pat my wet hands against my hot face and neck, mumble something about needing to cool off, and move to the corner farthest from him and closest to the door. Sitting on the floor on the other side of the gym bag, I try to do what I do best: disappear.

Most of my life I've felt invisible. In fact, I kind of like it that way. There are no threats or expectations, no misunderstandings, no mistakes when you're just watching. I love to read life. From afar, that is. Body language. The sounds or smells of a setting. How all the pieces come together, or how they symbolize something bigger. It's like I'm there, but not really, so my brain is free to read all those details other people probably miss. Ms. Carter said that's why my own writing is so strong. I soak up what I see and put it in my stories. I've got about twenty notebooks full of them. Not that anyone ever reads them, except for Ms. Carter. I've shown her a few. That was the first time I ever felt like maybe I wanted to be seen. Maybe I wanted to be heard. That maybe, in some small way, I mattered too.

Now I wish I hadn't shown her. Not because she said they were terrible. No, Ms. Carter did something worse—she said they were amazing. Riveting. That's the word she used. She told me that I had a great voice, original ideas, and, worst of all, that I should apply to UBC's Creative Writing Program. I wish she hadn't told me that. Because I would not have dared to dream it otherwise. I would not have made a portfolio or filled out an application. I would not have gotten the e-mail that arrived yesterday from the University of British Columbia, the one that that broke my heart.

I could blame Ms. Carter for that. But really, it's my fault, for getting my hopes up. I should have known better. I should have stayed invisible.

The e-mail.

I remember now. I had just left Writer's Craft class for my appointment with Mrs. Goodwin, my guidance counselor, when Mr. Wilson called the lockdown. Just as well, I figured. I'd printed the e-mail from UBC to show her. I knew she'd want to talk about it. But really, why bother? How was sitting in Mrs. Goodwin's office, sucking on a Lifesaver, squirming under the weight of her concerned gaze, going to make any difference? Pity is the last thing I need. Or want. Besides, talking won't change anything. I am not going to UBC.

But by the time I got back to class, Ms. Carter was in full lockdown mode. Lights out. Door locked. She'd even covered the long rectangular window with her Snoopy poster: "Be the author of your own life." I knocked anyway, called out, jostled the handle only to hear shuffling, giggling, shushing—but no one let me in. They were gathered in the dark corner trying to make each other laugh. Trying to secretly text their friends doing the exact same thing in every other room. That door wasn't opening until the police or the principal unlocked it. And getting caught by them, out there like that, would not only ruin Principal Wilson's perfect lockdown drill record, but also my invisible life. I could just imagine being the lockdown loser—the butt of everyone's jokes. Bad enough my own class was laughing at me, I didn't need the whole school mocking me, too.

I remember trying the door to the women's washroom in the far corner down the hall. I banged on the locked door a few times but no one opened it either. At the other end of the hall, the stairwell handle clanged as someone pulled on the latch and, instinctively, I lunged for the next door on the other side of me. MEN. Vandalized, just like every men's room door here, with a helmet drawn in red Sharpie on the man icon standing beside the wheelchair one, and that big red X before the word MEN. But I hardly gave it—or the fact that I was resorting to the men's room—a second thought. I needed to hide.

I shoved the door—relieved to feel it give way as I blundered in. I barely glimpsed the red bag by the entrance as I tripped over it, or the marble sink on the right that I tried to avoid as I fell. But the last thing I saw before slamming my head was what surprised me most: a six-foot, 250-pound rabbit in a plaid vest, standing at a urinal.

"I remember now," I say, clearing my throat. "I did trip coming in."

Absorbed by her tiny screen, Isabelle completely ignores me.

Indifferent, the Hulk flicks his ash on the floor.

Just as well. I'm not looking to be noticed by either of them. Especially him. But I can't help but wonder: What is his story. Where do all those rumors come from? And if Isabelle hadn't come in . . . what would he have done? My mind pulls at threads, trying to weave his story in a way that doesn't leave my stomach in knots.

We've been in here just a few minutes and it already feels like a lifetime. Maybe I'm picking up on their feelings—his anger or her irritation. Sometimes my empathy overwhelms me. Or maybe it's just a mashup of my fears: being trapped . . . feeling exposed and vulnerable. Antsy, that's the word. Either way, I want out. Now. If only there were a DRINK ME bottle or an EAT ME cake. A magic mirror. A tiny door—I'd take it. I'd take anything over this.

Poor Noah. This must be how he feels most of the time. I hug my legs and rest my forehead on my knees. Ten more minutes. I can do ten more minutes in here, can't I?

I reason it through. Isabelle has a phone. Worst-case scenario, we call for Mr. Wilson to come let us out first in his drill rounds. Surely he will, if Isabelle Parks asks. Besides, most drills only last about fifteen minutes, and if Noah can do it, so can I.

I think about my brother. Period 4 is his quiet time with Kim. And even though she's absent today, the supply educational assistant is with him. There's space in the High Needs room—much more than in here. Books to keep him quiet. Of the two of us, I'd say Noah is the lucky one.

For a change.

NOAH

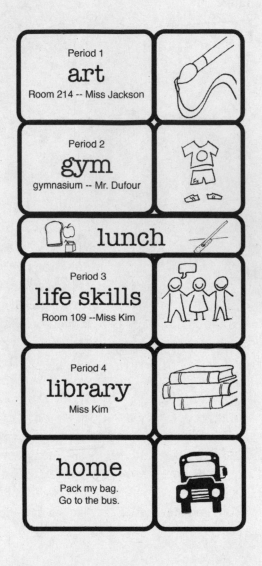

Period 1
art
Room 214 -- Miss Jackson

Period 2
gym
gymnasium -- Mr. Dufour

lunch

Period 3
life skills
Room 109 --Miss Kim

Period 4
library
Miss Kim

home
Pack my bag.
Go to the bus.

HOGAN

I stub the joint on the tile and flick it at the wall. With a ping, it ricochets off the rusty towel box beside Izzy. She looks up, disgusted, and just goes back to her texting.

Man, I'd give anything to have her see me like she did that day back in grade 10. When I scored that touchdown. When I felt like I could do almost anything because of how she looked at me—like I was awesome. Because of her, I believed it too.

And at the bush party later that night, how she sat next to me on the log and leaned in. Man, she was beautiful. Hair swept high in a ponytail, firelight glowing on the curve of her neck. Her face warm. And her eyes dark and sparkling as she smiled at me. I just wanted to kiss her—and next thing, I did. Isabelle Parks—the girl every guy wanted. And she wanted me. Hogan King.

I wish I could go back two years. Back to that night. And stay there. Forever.

Before everything happened. Before I was this loser, stinking of weed and sweat in a mangy Value Village reject costume, sitting on the bathroom floor.

Oh ya, Hulkster, she must find you irresistible now.

I got a glimpse of what it must be like for guys like Darren Greene or my brother Randy. But who am I kidding? That kind of life, that kind of love—it's not for me.

After Randy died, everything changed. Nothing matters any more. Mom and Dad. Teachers. Wilson. Everyone looks at me like I'm a problem. A problem they can't solve. The ones I never get on Hurley's math tests. Solve for X. I gave up trying to make sense of it. I gave up talking about it. They can ask the question fifty different ways but sometimes X is just a dumb X. Nothing more.

Once a loser, always a loser.

"That's my last one," I say to her, nodding at the butt on the floor by her feet. I want her to know. "I'm done with that crap. Just so you know."

"Right."

"No, seriously. I'm done."

"Whatever, Hogan. It's your life. I don't care."

And the thing is, she doesn't. I can't get mad at her for that, even though I am. She did care once—I had my chance with her and I blew it. Hell, I've blown a million chances these past two years—with football, school, my job, my parents. Coach Dufour tried to kick me in the ass a few times. But he didn't get it. Even if I wanted to, I couldn't do anything but watch as it all went up in smoke.

It's like, whenever someone cares—I can't. When they believe there's still good in me, I go outta my way to prove them wrong. Because there can't be good in me. There isn't.

Not after what I've done.

Still, I made a promise to Coach not to buy any more weed. And I haven't. I won't. That doesn't mean I'm about to let this last one go to waste. It's not like I'm in training or anything. But if Dufour catches me, he'll kick me out of Outdoor Ed, and honestly, it's the only reason I come to school any more. Izzy's right. I do hate school; I'm probably failing everything—but I like Coach's class. When we go out on the trails up in the Gatineau Hills, it's like I leave all that other crap behind. I blast my tunes, pump my legs until the sweat is dripping off me, just like I used to in football practice, and I feel myself rising above it all the more we climb. I swear, that is a high way better than any hit. Coach even brought in a mountain bike I could use when I said I didn't have one.

No pity. No judging. Not even after he found out what I did. He just brought in the bike. He's all right, Coach Dufour— because he isn't trying to make me into something I'm not.

The toilet flushes in the handicap stall and the girls both jump and look over at me with the same panicked expression. They must have figured it was just us in here. A couple seconds later, out comes that skinny guy in the black jeans and an X-Men T-shirt. With all the girl drama, I forgot he was in here—not to mention his weird entrance. He came blasting in while I was taking a leak. Just dropped his bag and made a beeline for the first stall. It's not every day you see a huge animal at a urinal, but this dude never even gave me a second glance. He sees me now, though, even though he's trying real hard not to.

Skinny Guy sets his ratty backpack and a camera on the floor by the sink while he washes his hands. I can tell by the way he avoids eye contact that he's freaked out by two girls in the bathroom. Or by being around girls at all, by the look of him. Probably been hiding in there waiting it out. Probably wanted to take a dump the whole time and couldn't. Not with them listening.

He washes his hands, a little longer than necessary, and I pick up his camera by the strap. It's a Canon. An old one by the look of it. Frayed strap. Cracked lens. The whole thing seems to be held together with gray duct tape.

"Don't!" Skinny Guy snatches the camera from me and quickly puts it around his neck. "You'll break it!"

And then, "Sorry," he adds, as if realizing exactly who he's talking to. "I just—I don't like people touching my stuff."

"Are you kidding me? Are you freaking kidding me right now?" Izzy stands, gawking at this dude. Like she can't believe he's here. I'm just glad to see it's not me that has set her off. She points at the door behind Nerd Girl. "There's, like, fifteen hundred people in this building. Three floors. A million rooms. And you choose mine?"

"Well, really you chose his," Nerd Girl blurts, then when we look her way, she retreats a bit and mumbles, "I mean, it is the men's room."

She's right. He was here first. And yet, somehow, in Izzy's mind all this is about her.

"What's your problem, Izzy?" I ask. Maybe it's a theater-kid thing but she's always been so overdramatic, even back in grade 7.

"My problem? MY problem? I don't have a problem." She points her finger at the guy, who has now squeezed himself into the far corner by the spilled garbage. "Why don't you ask Xander-freaking-Watt? Why don't you ask him what HIS problem is?"

She's pretty riled up. In fact, she seems almost afraid of Skinny Guy. I don't know why. She could take him. Hell, even scrawny Nerd Girl could.

"You are not allowed to be anywhere near me, you perv. That was the agreement."

He nods, but doesn't look up.

"Wilson said!" Her lips are trembling. Is she gonna cry?

"But you both take Writer's Craft," Nerd Girl says, poking her head up again. "Period 4. He's in your class. Our class."

One look from Izzy and she shrinks away.

"I needed the credit," Izzy says, turning back to him. "But Ms. Carter said we'd never have to work together. And the police warned you, Xander."

Police?

Now I'm really curious. This is more than just Izzy overreacting. I look at the guy trying to disappear in the corner. Pulling his legs in, his backpack close. Wrapping himself around that camera like a balled-up spider. There's gotta be more to this geek than I thought.

"Screw this!" Izzy blurts. "I am SO outta here." She moves towards the door, but Nerd Girl jumps up and blocks her.

"You can't leave . . . and, oh whoa, WHOA, WHOA!!" She twists the bolt. "People! This has to be locked!" She turns back, her eyes wide as she whispers, "We have to stay here. We have to be quiet."

"Get out of my way!" Izzy moves to shove her aside. "I don't have to do anything. It's just another stupid drill. No one—"

Izzy's phone buzzes in her hand and she glances down.

"But those are the rules," Nerd Girl continues. "We stay until the officer unlocks the door and it is over. It won't be much longer. Most lockdown drills are over in, like, fifteen minutes and—"

"Guys." Surprisingly, Izzy takes a step back. I thought for sure she'd blow by her. But instead, she looks up from her phone, her face white. Her voice a whisper, she says, ". . . it's not a drill."

ISABELLE

BRI: OMG NOT A DRILL!
Overheard Wilson and cops.
There's like five of them now and more coming.
They said there's a SHOOTER in the building!!!
A SHOOTER!!!
He shot out the atrium display cases.
OMG IZZY NOT A DRILL!

IZZY: SHOT?! Like with a GUN?!

BRI: I'll txt if I hear anything else
OMG I can't stop shaking.
What if he comes in the office?
What if he finds me?

IZZY: Stay hidden. Stay quiet.
No one knows you're there.
Just stay where you are.

ALICE

I read about stuff like this in the news—shootings, guns, real lockdowns.

But it doesn't happen here at St. Francis Xavier. Right? This can't be really happening.

The text has to be part of the prank. Yes. That's probably it. That has to be it.

Isabelle returns to sit in the corner opposite Xander. Apparently, whatever threat he poses is less than the unknown danger outside that blue door. Her thumbs dart in a blur over her iPhone screen as she texts.

"Don't worry," the Hulk says. "It's just another Friday prank. Another stupid joke." But even he isn't sounding too convinced.

True, there have been many of those ridiculous pranks this past semester. Up until Mr. Wilson called the assembly about it, they seemed to be happening almost every other Friday. The X-Guys, or whoever they are, would pull the fire alarm sending the whole school out to the back field. Then, while the building was empty they'd stay back and set up their latest stunt. No one knew who they were, but we all knew their pranks: false alarms, stink bombs, exploding garbage cans. But the worst, by far, was when they destroyed the grad mural. Splattered the whole thing with red and yellow paint in their signature big X.

"It's not a joke. It's vandalism," I say, remembering how crushed I was when I saw the mural. It took the committee (me and Lucy Lowry) weeks to design our Tree of Knowledge, and weeks more to hand-letter every grad's name on a leaf. "That was supposed to be our grad legacy."

The Hulk shrugs. "Guess some people wanna be remembered in a different way."

"By pranks? Nice legacy," I mumble. When Grampa died this winter, he left behind Waters' Farm, the kennels, the dogs he bred and trained over the years, the happy families that adopted them, the Pet Therapy Program he started at the Children's Hospital—all the things Gran and I are trying to carry on. Now that is a legacy—something worth leaving behind.

Isabelle looks up from her phone. "Well, there are tons of better ways to be known and remembered than pranks or a mural." She flicks her gaze towards me. "No offense."

"What—like pep rallies?" the Hulk scoffs. "Sorry, but I'd rather be known for something other than wearing stupid Spirit Day crap."

"You are," she snaps, and folds her arms.

She seems insulted, but he's right. I mean, who wants to walk around school all day in a precariously pinned bedsheet? I'm sure a bunch of those togas were still warm off the mattress that morning. That's not fun. It's unsanitary.

"I guess some kids wanna leave St. F-it with a bang," the Hulk continues. "You know, make their mark in their own way."

We all look at him. Even Xander.

Isabelle eyes him skeptically. "You don't know anything about this . . . prank, do you, Hogan?"

For a moment, he seems almost hurt by her accusation. But the scowl quickly returns, drops over the hurt like a mask. Like the Hulk is unable to control a bit of Bruce Banner from breaking out now and then.

"What?" she says defensively. "You do have a record. I'm just saying."

"For stealing. One stupid Supercycle from Canadian Tire." He sneers in disgust. "It's bad enough it cost me my placement there, my co-op credit, a month's grounding, AND a criminal record. I needed that co-op credit to graduate."

"Technically, you did break the law," Xander adds, for no good reason whatsoever.

"I needed a bike," the Hulk says, like that justifies everything. "So what? Now I'm guilty of being a psycho? Nice. Thanks, Izzy. Thanks a lot."

"That's not what I meant and you know it." She defends herself so hotly, I wonder if she really does feel bad for bringing it up. "I was just . . . just pointing out the facts."

"Can't argue with fact," Xander adds, unhelpfully.

"Well, how about I point out a few facts about you?" The Hulk spits the words. "Little Miss Perfect driving Mommy's BMW to soccer practice. And horseback riding. And dance competitions. And drama-geekfests. I wanna horse. I wanna cruise. I wanna iPhone."

A flush spreads up her neck and cheeks and she quietly slips her phone into her back pocket.

"Little Miss Perfect who gets any toy, any trip . . . and any guy she wants," he continues. "John, Trev, Darren. Sounds like you've got a record of your own."

"What?" She frowns as she searches for the words. "I'm not . . . I don't . . ."

"So do you just order boyfriends—like some kinda drive-thru? 'Gimme a tall blond.' 'I'll try a grande bold, black.' Or do you just go for the special of the month, like your fancy tai chi?"

Chai tea, I correct, pleased that I manage to keep that one inside my head.

He has a point. She does do all of those things, right down to the Starbucks. But that is just Isabelle. Isabelle Parks—the chosen one. School President. Yearbook Editor. MVP. Isabelle Parks not only knows all about the school, she runs it. In her mind, she is St. F.X. High School. She often comes late to class because she stops at the drive-thru on her spare. Had I the car or money to buy a coffee every day, or the nerve to always come late to class, I would at least bring one in for Ms. Carter. But it never seems to occur to Isabelle that she is interrupting us each time she arrives late. I guess, in her egocentric universe, nothing starts until she arrives. No lesson. No meeting. No practice. No performance. If she thinks of us at all, which she obviously doesn't, she must assume that we just sit around in nothingness waiting for her appearance. Like she is the Big Bang.

But I never take it personally. Everything in Isabelle's life is about Isabelle. She is the center of her universe and that of her parents, her friends, and every guy who has ever been infatuated with her. Their worlds revolve around her.

So she has both parents. So what? So they are rich lawyers. So she has the time and talent to excel at whatever she tries. Sure we envy her for it. Wonder what it would be like to be that dark-haired girl standing on stage bathed in a spotlight and drowned in applause. Who wouldn't? But I've never seen anyone react like the Hulk. Like he sees her successes as inversely proportional to his own. Like she does it to spite him.

"Shut up, Hogan," she finally says, eyes brimming. "You don't know anything about me. So just shut it."

Click.

Xander's shutter stops her short. She glares at where he sits, face hidden behind the lens.

"Did you . . .?" She wipes her eyes. "Ohmigod, did you seriously just take a picture of me right now?!"

Click.

Xander takes another, catching the exact moment her pain flares into anger.

"What the hell?!" She stands and looks at her face in the cracked mirror as she runs her finger under her eyes to wipe the mascara smudge. "I told you before. Wilson told you. You can't just go around taking random pictures like that!"

An overreaction. Even for Isabelle.

"Why not?" I ask, curious now. As Yearbook Editor she rarely went anywhere without her camera. "You take pictures all the time." Not that I am ever in any of them. Still, I don't know why she is reacting so strongly. "I assumed you liked having your picture taken . . . given all your selfies on Instagram and Facebook."

"Oh, so now you're creeping me?" She raises her eyebrows and put her hands on her hips, challenging me.

"Um, no," I say, unsure if it is creeping, exactly. I am sorry I spoke. Why did I speak? Nothing good ever comes of it. "It's just . . . we are friends."

"Friends?" She looks at me like I just articulated the ridiculous.

"On Facebook, I mean."

"Oh. That. So, not like real-real friends."

Real-real friends?

"Well," I say, "it's not like you're my imaginary friend. Although I did have one of those when I was younger—"

"Whatever." Thankfully, she cuts me off. "I have, like, 1,523 Facebook friends and almost 1,800 followers on Instagram." She turns back to the mirror and fixes her perfect hair. "I can't be expected to know them all."

"But you know me, right?" I blurt. I mean, she does. She has to. "We went to elementary school together since kindergarten?

Remember? I invited you to my last birthday party back in grade 4?"

Everything comes out like a question. But I know the answer. My face burns.

"C'mon, Izzy," the Hulk jeers, enjoying my awkward moment. He gestures at me with his furry arm. "What's her name?" Like he knows. I doubt he does. I hope he doesn't.

She looks at me then, as if willing herself to remember. But the truth is, she can't. "I know of you," she brags, like that is something. "You're . . . that guy's sister Allie, right?"

"It's Alice, actually," I mumble, recalling that she did not come to that birthday party because, as she told me then, "Your brother is too weird."

But even my words get lost as she turns to the Hulk. "See?" She smiles triumphantly. "I do know who she is."

XANDER

Writer's Craft Journal

Xander Watt

February 4, 2016

PROMPT: If you could only save one thing in a fire, what would that be?

Facts: July 25, 2011—Mom's Matinée cigarette fell onto the living room carpet and started to smolder. The fire alarm woke me at 1:25 a.m., and when I saw the smoke and flames, I called 9-1-1. The operator told me to get everyone out. In the 13 minutes it took the fire truck to get to our house, I not only helped Mom onto a lawn chair out front, as well as Sheldon, my turtle, I also rescued the three crates of Dad's comics collection I carried up from the basement, my box of 151 original Pokémon guys, my Lego Death Star that Dad and I were working on, and even a box of Ritz crackers in case Mom and I got hungry. The firemen arrived at 1:38 while I was standing on the porch in my Darth Vader PJs. Back to the flames, camera in hand, I looked through the lens at all I had saved that night.

Mom, slumped in her Blue Jays lawn chair, surrounded by all our most important things. I'd put hers in her lap: her big, red purse, her near empty bottle of Jackson-Triggs wine, her pack of Matinée cigarettes.

Click.

The lighting was perfect. Excellent composition. It still is one of my most favorite pictures. Mom thanked the firemen for saving our house that night. I thought she would have been happy with all I did, but when she saw that photo, she only cried.

I was twelve, just a kid, really, but I realized four things on July 25:

1. Anyone can save more than one thing in a typical house fire.

2. Though she's always looking for them, apparently, Mom's purse, Matinée cigarettes, and Jackson-Triggs wine are NOT her favorite things.

3. Had I not called 9-1-1 (like I was supposed to) and not evacuated (like I was supposed to), I probably could have peed on the carpet (like I'm not supposed to) and put the fire out.

4. Dad really wasn't coming back home. Not for his comics. Not for his camera. And not for me.

So to answer your illogical question, if I had to pick just one thing, I'd pick my camera. It's a Canon T90, a manual focus 35 mm SLR. Nicknamed "the Tank" by Japanese photojournalists because of its ruggedness. Like me, it can endure a lot of things. Plus the T90 is voted by experts as the best Canon design ever—even if newer models are preferred by other photographers.

And my dad.

HOGAN

The awkward silence after the name-that-girl gongshow doesn't last long.

Unfortunately.

I'm not one for talk and these girls never shut up. Xander's weird and all. And kinda obsessed with that picture thing. But at least he's quiet. Minds his own business.

"They're not answering." Izzy's thumbs tick-tick-tick across the phone. "Why won't they answer?"

"Oh, so everyone has to jump when you call?" I say.

"Who?" Alice asks.

"Darren or Bri," Izzy says. "She's hiding in the main office. But I haven't heard from Darren since before the lockdown."

"Well," Alice goes, "it's against the rules to text in a lockdown."

I'm not a rule follower, but still, this isn't some drill. Or some prank. Something's not right. I feel it in my gut. "What's the point of hiding from a psycho shooter if their phones keep buzzing with your stupid texts?"

"Psycho shooter?" She looks at me, horrified, then back at the phone.

Alice nods. "Well, clearly, anyone who brings a gun to a school is unstable." She starts mumbling about stats in the news.

I'm not sure why I keep giving Izzy such a hard time. All that crap about being a princess. About the guys she's dated. I'm jealous of Darren. I admit it. But why the digs about remembering Alice's name, and, now, freaking her out about her texts? Hurting Izzy? That's the last thing I want to do. But things get all jumbled in my head and come out the wrong way, and they usually end up sounding like the exact opposite of what I mean. Honestly, I was trying to reassure her. No. That's not it, exactly. What I really want is for her to stop texting and pay attention to me. But it seems the only attention I know how to get is for being an ass.

And I am a master at that. Just to prove it (and in part to stop Alice from freaking everyone out with her gunmen trivia) I kick Xander's foot. "So, loser. Tell us what you did that's got Izzy so freaked out? Did you take her picture or something?"

He stops messing with his camera and looks at me in surprise. Like he's just realized I'm in the room. Or where he is. Total spacer.

"Hogan!" Izzy snaps. "Why don't you just mind your own busin—"

"Was she naked? She totally was!" That must be it. I mean, why else would she be so riled up about it? "Were you stalking her through the bedroom window?"

I see it all play out in my imagination. It's pretty sweet.

"No," Xander mumbles. "The door was open and I saw her—"

"Shut! Up!" Izzy cuts him off.

"Dude," I go, "you could make some serious coin with those." I know I'd pay to see them. What guy wouldn't?

Alice is completely bug-eyed. "That's child pornography! You know that, right? A criminal offense. Even if you don't pay for it, even if it's e-mailed and you just forward it, you could be implicated. Don't you remember what Officer Scott said? In that Social Media Safety presentation about—"

"I wasn't naked!" Izzy yells.

I look at Xander and he shakes his head. Now I'm really curious. "So . . . what, then?"

He opens his mouth.

"I swear to God, Xander." Izzy points at him. "If you say one word about it, you're dead."

His face goes pale, like she's waving a machete and not a manicured finger. His mouth snaps shut.

So much for that.

"But you guys know that, right?" Alice continues with her public service announcement. Totally killing my buzz. "About naked pictures? Because a teenager is legally a minor. So, even if I forwarded a photo like that in a text, I'd be liable. And—"

"Yeah, we get it!" Izzy interrupts. "I don't think you have anything to worry about. People sending you naked photos, Alice? Is that, like, a real-life true-drama problem for you?" Izzy looks at her with that face. The one I thought she saved for me. The one that says: God, you're an idiot. "Do you, like, even have a phone?"

"Um, no. Well, not exactly," Alice says. "My Gran has a flip phone—"

"A flip phone?" Izzy laughs. Alice might as well have said she uses a banana phone. I mean, I don't have a phone either. But only because I lost it. Three times. At least when I have one it's the latest model.

"Yeah." Alice laughs, but her face doesn't.

"How do you text? Or check e-mail? Or take pictures? It's like you're living in the 1980s."

Alice shrugs like it's no big deal. "I never really . . . I dunno. I guess, I just don't need a phone."

"Oh, right. I get it." Izzy nods condescendingly. "I mean, no offense, but who are you gonna call?"

"GHOST . . . BUSTERS!" Xander explodes. We all stop and stare at him. A look of panic crosses his face. "You know?" And then, he starts to sing, like that'll help. "Some-thin' strange . . ." He's nodding and waving his hand for us to join in. "In your neigh-bor-hood . . . Who you gonna call?"

Silence.

Xander's lips part like he's showing his teeth to the dentist. I think he's trying to smile. Or something. It's just weird.

"Something strange is right," I say.

His mouth closes and he looks back at his camera. "Ray Parker, Jr.," he mutters. "From the soundtrack. I have the 45."

"SUCH a loser," Izzy says, cutting him off.

"It's a movie," Alice explains. "About a trio of spirit exterminators. I think it's from the 80s."

"Well, you would know." Izzy sighs dramatically as she returns to her phone. "Could this day get any worse?"

I wish she hadn't asked that. Because it always can.

At least, for me, it always does.

ISABELLE

BRI: Sorry, couldn't reply. Trying to hear what Wilson and the cops are saying in his office.
There's like five of them here now and more on the way.

IZZY: Do they know who it is?

BRI: Don't think so.

IZZY: Are you ok to txt? I don't wanna get you in trouble.
Or draw attention with the buzzing.

BRI: On mute. ;)

Txting is my lifeline. Seriously.
This whole thing is INSANE.
I can't stop shaking.
You doing ok?

IZZY: Ya if you think being stuck in a washroom with Hogan and Xander Watt is ok.

BRI: ?? Xander is there too?

IZZY:	Yep. Shoot me now. Sorry. :/ . . . you know what I mean.
BRI:	It's like your worst nightmare.
IZZY:	No kidding. Get this. He's already taken two pics of me!!!
BRI:	Seriously?? WTF? What about Wilson's "behavior contract"? Isn't it supposed to be like some restraining order—no more pics of you?
IZZY:	Kind of. Wilson made him destroy mine.
BRI:	I never did see them. How bad could they be? You look amazing all the time.
IZZY:	Bad. Believe me.
BRI:	They should've done more than just kick him out of Yearbook class.
IZZY:	He never should have been in it in the first place. He never edited the grad write-ups. And his pics were just . . . weird. People pay $60 for a yearbook, they want pics of GOOD memories.
BRI:	Like hot football players.
IZZY:	EXACTLY! Teams winning. High-fives. Spirit Week.
BRI:	Friends hanging out and having fun.
IZZY:	Not creeper shots of breakups, loners eating lunch, or druggies lighting up.
BRI:	Seriously. Who wants to see that?
IZZY:	I had to do all my work AND his to meet the deadline.
BRI:	What's he doing now?
IZZY:	Just sitting there. Zooming in and out on the floor. OBSESS much??
BRI:	Effed up. Loser.

XANDER

Writer's Craft Journal

Xander Watt

February 18, 2016

ASSIGNMENT: read the poem "Ellie: An Inventory of Being" and write one in a similar form about yourself. Explore and express those inner conflicts as concisely as you can.

I am Xander.

I am seventeen years old.
Mom calls me Alexander.
Grandpa can't remember what to call me.
Dad just never calls.

I am sometimes ignored,
often forgotten,
mostly invisible—
but it's no superpower.

I don't know how to talk to girls.
I don't get them
so I don't get them.
But that's okay because, like all strange and unusual creatures,
they both intrigue and terrify me.

I think too much sometimes,
blurt the wrong thing often, and
feel confused, always.

I do Social Autopsies,
dissecting my awkward conversations
to determine the exact
cause of death.

I want to finish the Lego Death Star I started when I was nine.
But I'm still missing a key piece—
my dad.

I am anti-Superman
and pro-Marvel.
I like a hero with a troubled past.
I guess, it gives me hope.

I wish life unfolded in graphic panels,
logical boxes of daily drama
narrated by Stan Lee or George Lucas.
A world where thoughts were clear and bold
in big bubbles overhead.

Then I'd get it.
I'd get you.
Because we are all just comic characters, really.
All of us villainous heroes or heroic villains
depending on the day.

I wonder what my life's mission will be?
Where will I boldly go?

But first, I need to fix some broken things.
Like my cracked camera lens.
My Lego Death Star.
And my family.

My name is Xander and this is me in 2016.

00:48:56

ALICE

I feel bad for Xander. He really has no clue. Conversations are like skipping double-dutch—completely confusing, next to impossible to enter, and mastered only by the cool girls, like Isabelle. She was the double-dutch queen back at St. Daniel's. Double-dutch, like a conversation, can look really confusing at first with so much going on in two directions, but if you watch closely, find the rhythm, and pace yourself, you just might be able to jump in.

Theoretically.

Timing is everything. So is how you enter. And leading with something like a terrible rendition of obscure lines from an '80s song is a sure way to kill a conversation. Jump in with that and just watch lines of communication drop dead around you.

Believe me, I know. Too bad Xander doesn't.

I never was able to get the hang of double-dutch even though I spent most grade 4 and 5 recesses as an ever-ender. Watching. Waiting. Wishing.

Well, at least until they replaced me with the flagpole.

Thankfully, no one is talking now. It's a lockdown, for heaven's sake! We're not supposed to make any noise at all. Bad enough that we aren't in our classes. Or that we didn't even have the door locked at first! Need I remind them, this isn't just a drill? (Maybe I do. They obviously forgot all about the Social Media Safety presentation.)

Rules exist for a reason. I know all about living with rules and, especially, the chaos that happens when they are ignored.

"There's, like, five cops downstairs and more coming," Izzy says. Thankfully, she's keeping her voice down. "What are they waiting for? Why aren't they just going after him?"

The Hulk leans his head back against the wall and closes his eyes. "After who, exactly?"

"Duh! The shooter," she says. "What are they waiting for?"

"Well," he adds, not opening his eyes, "if an armed posse is sweeping the halls, it's probably smart to first get some idea of who they're looking for. There's fifteen hundred people in this building. He could be anyone. How are they gonna know which one to arrest?"

She frowns for a second. "Well, he's the one with the gun, obviously!"

"Oh, right. He's just sitting there waiting for them to come and find him." He smirks. "It's not some hide-and-seek game, Iz. The guy probably has some kind of plan."

I don't like the sound of that.

"It's common sense," the Hulk continues. "They need to know as much as they can about the guy before they start shooting everything that moves."

"Is that what they do?" I ask, aghast.

"All the kids and teachers are locked down," Isabelle says. "Anyone out in the hall is clearly the perp."

"Pfffft!" the Hulk chides. "The perp. Listen to you. You think binge-watching HBO cop shows makes you an authority on policing?"

"Oh, and petty theft does?"

"Guys, guys," I remind them, "we really shouldn't be talking." I glance at the blue door. "I mean, he could be right outside."

"We're fine," the Hulk says. "For all we know the guy took off after he trashed the atrium displays. It's just anoth—"

BANG!

We jump at the explosive sound still ringing in the hall outside. Even the Hulk sits bolt upright and glances warily at the door.

"Is that a gunshot?" Isabelle whispers hysterically. "It's him! It's him! He's right outside our door!"

BANG-BANG-BANGBANG!

Isabelle screams. Or maybe I do as I cower at the sound, hands over my ears. But nothing stops the thud-thud-thudding of my heart. Another shriek. This time I know it's not me. Or Isabelle. The scream is coming from outside the washroom, fading with the footsteps as someone runs down the hall.

I go numb. It can't be. It can't.

But it is.

I'd know that wail anywhere. And though everything in my body says hide, I push my back into the wall, dig my feet into the floor, and drive my shaky legs to straighten and stand.

"Ohmigodohmigod, we're gonna die!" Isabelle rocks slightly as the Hulk moves over and puts his arm around her.

"You're okay. We're safe in here and no one is getting in," he whispers, as he rubs her back, trying to comfort her. I move towards the door. "That's probably just the police," he says. "If they've found him, it's gonna be over soon."

He's probably right. And that is exactly why I have to go out.

HOGAN

Alice moves to the door. What the hell is she doing?

The panic on her face is clear as she looks at the bolt and back at me and Izzy. "I have to go out there."

"What?" I jump up and join her. "Are you nuts?" I whisper. "Five minutes ago you're obsessing like some crazy bylaw officer: lock the door, no talking, no texting. And now, you want to leave?"

She unlocks the deadbolt with a thunk.

I slap my hand on the door, holding it shut. "Listen. Maybe there is nothing to worry about. Like I said, it's probably some lame prank. But use that nerd-brain of yours, Alice. The fact is some nutjob is out there with a gun. A GUN!"

She heaves on the handle, but it won't budge. "Please!" She pulls with all her puny strength. "That is exactly why I have to go out there."

"What about the rules?"

"It's Noah." She looks at me with desperate eyes. "That was

him screaming. He's out there somewhere. Don't you get it? Noah needs me." She tugs on the handle. "You have to let me go. Please! I have to help my brother."

My hand falters at the word "brother," and just like that—she yanks the door open just enough to squeeze through.

Crouched, she scurries down the side of the hallway, stopping to listen every few feet. For her prey. For her predator. Just like a small mouse.

"OhmiGOD! What are you doing?" Izzy whispers, pushing on the door as I watch Alice kneel by the corner at the far end of the hall. "Are you, like, insane?! Shut it! Shut it! Lock it! Lock it!"

Xander doesn't move. "I wouldn't go out there if I were you," he says. Like he knows what I'm considering. Hell, I don't even know.

No, wait, I do.

I'm thinking about Randy. About how helpless I felt watching the blood, so much blood, spill out of my brother's head on the gray tiles.

And it was all your fault.

I'm thinking about how I would've given anything, done anything, to save him. I'm thinking Alice has a ton of nerve, that little Nerd Girl. And heart. And absolutely no common sense at all.

And without thinking any more, I fling open the door and run after her.

Lockdown Social Story

When there is a LOCKDOWN the teacher will

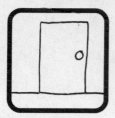

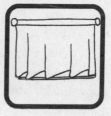

LOCK
the door,

turn OFF
the lights,

and COVER
the windows.

Students stay in the classroom.
Everyone must be QUIET.
NO TALKING allowed in a lockdown.

Wait quietly until
Principal Wilson or a police officer
opens the door.

Not the room.
Not the room.
Not the right room.

Ha-KU-na Ma-TA-ta!
Ha-KU-na Ma-TA-ta!
Ha-KU-na Ma-TA-ta!

ISABELLE

He left me? He left me! Ohmigod!

How could Hogan just leave me? Now? In here with him?

For a moment, I think about running after Hogan and Alice. I even crack open the door and check down the hall.

Empty.

Screw you, Hogan! How could you be so selfish? What about me?

Who knows where they are now, or the gunman, for that matter? I close the door and lock it. Xander is sitting in the corner with his damn camera.

Better the psycho I know than the one I don't, I guess.

I hope.

"Don't get any ideas," I say, moving to the corner farthest from him.

He blinks. "I get ideas all the time. How do you stop yourself from—?"

"I mean stay over there. And no pictures."

He nods.

I check my phone. Still no word from Darren. I send another text. Why isn't he answering?

Maybe his phone is dead. I don't let myself think beyond that. I can't or I'll lose it completely.

This can't be happening. It can't.

And yet, it is.

"Could this day get any worse?" I mutter.

"Why do you always ask that?" Xander says. "It is an odd question. I mean, wouldn't it make more sense to ask how it might get better?"

True. With an armed psycho on the loose, it definitely might get worse. Much worse. "Whatever."

Nervously, I fiddle with my woven bracelet, spinning its knot around my wrist.

"Did you make that?" he asks.

"No," I say, not really wanting to talk to him, of all people. But I need the distraction. "It was a gift. From my DR mom. She made it for me."

"What's a DR mom?"

"You know, the DREX team?"

He shakes his head. How has he not heard of DREX? We've been fundraising, like, all year. The cake auction. The dance. Hello? "Dominican Republic Experience team? A bunch of us went to the DR."

"Like, at a resort?"

I snort. "No, this was nothing like a resort. We stayed with the locals and visited the sugarcane fields, the orphanage. Stuff like that. You know, see what their life is really like. Anyway, Teresa, the mother at the house that billeted me, she gave me this when I left."

Teresa. I smile a bit, just thinking about her and her family. Even though I was only with her for ten days, honestly, it was the closest thing I ever felt to being truly mothered. We barely spoke each other's language and yet, from the moment she welcomed me off the bus and into her home, I felt like she knew me. Really knew me. Really cared, anyway.

"Oh, so you were helping the poor," he says.

"Sort of . . . well, we gave them school supplies and stuff. But I feel like I learned so much from them."

I've been home two weeks, and I still can't even put that trip into words. Miss Sweeney, one of the teacher supervisors, suggested we journal. But all the things I saw, the injustice, the poverty, men laboring in the sugarcane fields, women working in the sweatshops, orphans—God, the orphans—there are no words. Not really.

I shrug and spin the bracelet round and round and round. "I dunno. But I've felt . . . different since I came back."

"Are you sick?" Xander asks. "You don't look sick."

"No. But my real mother thinks I caught a bug of some kind."

She's been on my case ever since I got home a few weeks back. She keeps telling me, "You're not acting like yourself." Shopping. Pedicures. Partying—it just doesn't interest me any more. All that stuff that mattered so much before I left—having more, being more, just to impress more—it just seemed so trivial, so ridiculous when I got home. My mother asked if I'd taken all of my malaria pills. Did I drink their water? "This is your final year, Isabelle!" she ranted. "I should never have let you go on that trip. You can't afford to be sick, not now, not when it's all about the grades."

For my mother, it is always about marks. My whole purpose in life is making the grade. And hers, apparently, is about making me make it.

"I'm just sick of my mother always being on my case," I blurt. "Now it's about acceptance letters. It's my life! Why can't I just do what I want to do?"

The outburst catches me by surprise. Why am I telling this to Xander Watt, of all people? But in some ways, it's so easy. He has no expression. No judgment. And I really don't care what he thinks anyway. Kinda like telling it to a robot.

He blinks. "What do you want to do?"

His question catches me off guard.

"I just . . . I just want to . . ." I heave a sigh. "I dunno. No one's ever asked me before. All I know is this trip changed everything. All the things I used to think were so important—aren't. Not any more." I shrug and look down at my bracelet, admit what I've been wondering these past few weeks. "Maybe I'm depressed."

But he doesn't look at me all judgey. "What does your mom think?"

I laugh, but it's not funny. "Yeah, I can only imagine the total freakshow if I ever told her I felt depressed. In my house, we don't heal scars, we hide them. Because if her kid is messed up, that means she messed up. And my mother never makes mistakes, never loses a case, never fails at anything. Ever."

We sit in silence.

"You're like my blue Hanes," he says.

"Your what?"

"Hanes. My underwear," he says, all matter-of-fact. "They were my favorite pair."

And suddenly I'm sorry I ever spoke. Xander Watt? Pfft! What was I thinking? Of course he's gonna get all inappropriate and stupid. It's what he does.

"I wore them all the time," he goes. "Mom even washed them out each night so I could wear them again the next day."

I don't want to know. I really don't. But I can't help myself. "What—like, you only owned one pair of underwear?"

"Oh, no. I have lots. But I don't like tags. And the waistband should have a certain elasticity. And sometimes the seams on the other pairs make my testicles—"

"Okay, okay." I throw my hands up. "I get it. These are your favorite pair. So what?"

"Well, I guess they got caught in the spinner or something and got totally stretched out. Just like you."

I raise my eyebrow at him. "Hello? Did you just compare my life to your nasty-ass underpants?"

"Yes." He nods, like it makes total sense. "It's a metaphor. A metaphor is when you—"

"I know what a metaphor is!" God! I'm so irritated to be caught up in his nonsense. "I just don't know why I bothered to listen to yours."

He shrugs and looks down at his camera strap. "Well, it makes sense to me. The DREX stretched you out. You can't go back to the way things were. No matter how much you want to." He nods, sure of it. "You're just like my blue Hanes."

I want to make some sharp comeback. To laugh him off. But as I watch him fiddling with his camera strap, not looking at me at all, I actually start to see some sense in his words. Life is about stretching yourself, I guess. And once your heart has been expanded there's no going back.

My parents, Bri, Darren—none of them get what I've been trying to say. I don't even get it myself. But Xander Watt does. Go figure.

"You know, Xander, in some weird way, that's, like, the wisest thing anyone's said to me these past two weeks."

"Sometimes, you just know when it's time to let things go and move on, right?"

I smile a bit, suprised by this weird connection. Who knows? Maybe I've been misjudging this guy all along. "It's like, you gotta be open to change when you see the signs."

He nods again, completely serious. "Like skidmarks. Now there's a sure sign it's time to change."

ALICE

I peek around the corner down the locker-lined hallway. Empty. No Noah. And no shooter either, thank God. I sprint, ducking into the first doorway to catch my breath. I stop and listen. Nothing.

Moving doorway to doorway, I skirt up the hallway, sure I'll be caught any second. But none of that matters, Noah is out here, somewhere. I just know it.

He should be with Kim, the educational assistant who works most closely with him. Period 4—that's reading time in the High Needs room or the library. But in all the drama, I forgot that Kim is off sick today. And though Julie, her supply, is a nice enough lady who knows all about autism, she knows nothing about Noah. Because only someone who really knows my brother would know that he bolts.

I swallow and listen for his familiar noises, hearing nothing but my heart drumming in my ears.

Come on. Where are you, Noah?

There's no point in calling his name. It would draw the police—who would most certainly lock me down. Or the shooter—who would most probably shoot me down. My stomach twists. No, calling won't help. Besides, even if he hears me, Noah won't answer.

At the last doorway before the hall splits, I stop and strain to hear that familiar tune: "Hakuna Matata." Noah hums it over and over when he's in distress. Most people wouldn't recognize the song, or even recognize it as a song, but it's as clear to me as if he's calling my name. Whenever he has nightmares, feels anxious, or is simply getting overwhelmed by the crowds or sounds, he starts humming, moaning, and flapping his hands. Rocking. Head slapping. And, if he gets there, a full-on meltdown.

Thankfully, he hasn't had one of those in a while. A couple of months at least. The last time, Kim was away for the day and the supply EA that day wasn't picking up on his triggers. He had a meltdown so bad that afternoon that they called a Secure School. Kept the classroom doors locked while the whole High Needs team tried to rein him in and calm him down. The last thing he'd need at that point was hundreds of kids pushing by in the hallway after the bell rang.

I should have been there. I should have known. I could tell things weren't great that day when I stopped by the High Needs room on the main floor. I usually eat lunch there with him, but that day, I just dropped off his sandwich and juice. I had to meet Ms. Carter to go over my writing portfolio for that pointless application. He seemed agitated, unsettled as he paced the room, uninterested in the match-the-card game the supply EA had spread out on the table. He'll be okay, I told myself. Apparently, he wasn't.

That meltdown never would have happened if I'd been there. I knew it. Gran knew it, too. Even if she never voiced it. I could tell by the way she looked at me.

"You're not his guardian angel," Mrs. Goodwin said later when I sat in the guidance office in tears. "You can't be everywhere. You can't watch over him all the time."

Mrs. Goodwin was probably right. But so was Gran.

"You and I are all he has," she told me years ago, when he'd had a major meltdown in the elementary playground. When I learned I couldn't just watch or run away even when others did. When I realized that Noah isn't like the others kids and, because of that, neither am I. "If we don't watch out for poor Noah," Gran explained, "who will?"

Both are true. I have to watch over Noah even though I will often fail. But what kind of sister would I be if I didn't even try?

I bolt across the hallway and lean flat against the lockers at the intersection where the halls form a T. Straight ahead, on the right, the stairwell doors lead down to the atrium. On the left are the windows overlooking it. It's a great vantage point to see down three hallways at once—and also, I realize, completely exposed.

Then I hear it: HaKUna MaTAta. HaKUna MaTAta. HaKUna MaTAta.

It's so faint I think I might have imagined it. I want to hear it so badly I wonder if I have. But no, the song grows louder as I travel the empty hall. And I know where he is.

Of course! The janitor's closet!

Noah always helps the custodian after lunch. His job is to sweep the floor, and Noah takes it pretty seriously. Mr. Dean even gave Noah his own broom—a four-foot-wide, swivel-head thing that can clear three tiles wide in one shove. Whether it's the sensation of it against the tile, the repetitious motion, or the quiet time of them both pushing in tandem, Noah loves sweeping. It comforts him.

I grasp the door handle. Please be unlocked. The knob turns and I open the closet to find Noah moaning and rocking among the brooms and buckets. He's gripping his broom's handle—compulsively flicking the masking-tape tag marked

"NOAH." His orange Lion King hat is rolled down over his eyes and ears—a sure sign the world is just too overwhelming. He wears it that way a lot. Some days, I wish I had a hat of my own. A quick escape until the spotlight goes away and the crowd moves on. Until the teacher calls on someone else. Or the girls stop laughing. Until I am invisible again.

Noah's song continues, and though there's barely enough room for him to stand, he seems content. He's always liked a tight squeeze when things feel chaotic. If he's having a really bad day at home, I usually pile all the couch cushions on him and sit on top. "That's not normal," a friend said once when she came over. I didn't know what she meant. It was our normal. We did it all the time. I stopped inviting friends over after that—or maybe I had no friends to invite. But it doesn't matter, really. Like Gran says, so long as Noah has a good day, we all do. Actually, I don't know if that's true, exactly. But I do know that if Noah has a bad day, we all do.

I glance down the hallway on both sides, unsure of what to do next. There's still no sign of anyone else. But for how long? I try to squeeze in with him but there isn't room for both of us. The door won't shut, and the jostling pitches his moan up a notch.

Once again, I have written myself into a dead end. I always get these great ideas and excitedly plot from one point to the next.

Get out of the room. Find Noah. And . . .

And what?

As usual, I have no idea how to resolve it. Only this is the worst time for a creative block. Because I'm not abandoning some fictional character to his unfinished fate. This time, it's real. This time, it's Noah.

And I'm all he's got.

ISABELLE

BRI: How you holding up?

IZZY: Ok, I guess. You?

BRI: I can't believe this is real. Darren said it's like an episode of Cops.
They're searching the building now.

IZZY: Darren? He txted you?

BRI: Ya. Why?

IZZY: I've txted him this whole time—he hasn't answered!
I thought his phone was off or in his locker.
What did he say? Is he mad at me or something?

BRI: Actually, we didn't talk about you at all.

IZZY: Oh.
Well what did he say?

BRI: Just stuff about Kate's party. OMG it was crazy!

IZZY: You were there? I thought you weren't going?

BRI: No . . . you said you weren't going.

IZZY: You went without me? First Darren and now you?
WTF?!

BRI: Iz, you can't get mad at us for wanting to have fun.

IZZY: Whatever. Like getting falling down drunk is fun.
I'm not into that. Not any more.
So, what lucky bachelor did you end up with this time?
Please tell me you didn't get back with Todd.

BRI: No, I didn't.
What's up with you, anyway?
Even Darren says you haven't been the same since
your trip.

IZZY: I'm not. I'm all blue-Hanes-ed.

BRI: I don't get it.

IZZY: I know.

ALICE

"**N**oah?" I take his hand firmly but gently. It flutters in my grasp like a trapped bird but I don't let it go. I have to get him back to the washroom. It's the only option. Not ideal, but safer. At least we'll be together.

I pull the bottom of the broom handle slightly, sliding the rectangular head into the hall as I coax him out. "Noah. Come with me. It's time to sweep."

Noah doesn't speak, but he has lots to say to the few people who know how to listen. No, his body says. He pulls away. Rocking side to side. Tapping his head. Noah knows his schedule, the photos Kim uses to cue him for his next activity. Lunch is over. Caf duty is done. It's library time with Kim now. This isn't right and he knows it.

"Come on, Noah," I urge, slowly turning up his hat so he can see. He tilts his head, watches me in his peripheral vision, as usual. As much as I want him to, he never looks at me directly, but I know he is listening.

I push the broom head with my foot and he follows its handle out of the closet. His free fingers twiddle his hair, worrying the strands left around the bald spot behind his ear.

BANG!

Instinctively, I duck down, dragging Noah by the arm. The explosion came from the main stairwell. Close. Too close.

"MUTANTS RULE!" a guy's voice shouts before getting drowned out by a series of blasts.

BANG-BANG! BANG!

Noah shrieks and raises his arm, breaking free to cover his ears.

BANG-BANG!

The stairwell window explodes, raining shards of glass down the hall.

"NO!" I reach, grasping at Noah's track pants as he tries to bolt. "Stay with me! NOAH! Stay here!"

But it's all too much for him. And he runs, broom in hand, back the way I came, disappearing around the corner.

I take off after him, terrified his long stride has already taken him out of my reach. But as I turn right, I run headlong into something huge. Someone huge. And ricocheting off the barrel chest, I fall back to the ground among the broken glass.

I look up to see the Hulk towering over me. He's got my brother by the scruff of the neck. And no matter how Noah shrieks and flails, the Hulk holds fast.

I don't know whether to be terrified or thankful.

Then, with his free hand, the Hulk reaches down for me. "C'mon! Move!"

The three of us run back down the hall, circling wide by the west stairwell doors. We sprint for the men's room, slamming into one another as we hit the locked door.

"Open up!" the Hulk pounds on it with his huge fist.

"She can't open it," I say, breathless. "It's against the rules."

"C'mon, Izzy!" He pounds harder. "It's us. Open the damn door!"

A few pops echo in the empty hall. Not nearly as close as the last ones, but just as unnerving. Especially when we hear, "This is the police! Put down your weapon!"

The blasts continue and seem to be growing louder. Closer. Any second I expect to see gunmen come running around the far corner.

The Hulk looks at me and we both know, there's no way she's opening it now.

"Screw this!" he yells and lifts his huge furry foot. He kicks the door hard. Once. Twice. On the third, the wood splinters around the lock, and the door flies open to reveal Isabelle cowering and freaking in one corner. While in the other, Xander watches us all through the lens of his camera.

Click.

ISABELLE

"**O**hmigod!" I scream as they literally come barging in. I rush past them and try to close the door but the bolt is ripped free. Which means the door won't stay shut. Which means we're gonna die!

Great. Just freaking great! Could this day get any worse?!

I walk over and shove him in his stupid furry chest. "You broke the damn door!"

"Well, YOU wouldn't open it." He pushes me aside and heads to a stall.

"We are in a freaking lockdown! Tell him, Alice!" I look at her for her rule-following support but she's too busy trying to calm down her weirdo brother.

"Where the hell did he come from?" I ask, but no one answers. For all I know, he could be the one the cops are after.

I look back at Hogan, who has not gone into the stall but

instead has grabbed the door by the top and side and is literally trying to rip it off.

"So you just go around breaking doors for fun now?" I say. "Is that it?"

The metal groans and shrieks as he twists and pulls. Is he serious right now? I glance back through the open doorway down the hall. He's gonna get us killed.

I shout over the noise, "Why don't you just put up a sign that says, HEY, PSYCHO, WE'RE IN HERE!?"

"Who needs a sign," he snaps, "when we've got you screaming it at the top of your lungs?"

I cover my mouth.

With a metallic shriek the door rips free. I didn't think he could do it. But now that he has, I have no idea why. Hogan carries it to the entrance.

"That metal door is too small to fit there," I say. But that isn't his plan. Instead, he shuts the wooden door and, holding the metal one parallel to the floor, rams it against the wood, wedging it in between the door and the edge of the sink. Smart. Well, at least until he starts pounding on it with his thick fists.

BAM! BAM! BAM!

I roll my eyes. "Why don't you make, like, more noise?"

Alice cuts in, "How about we all make less?" She looks a bit frazzled. With a brother like that, who wouldn't? He's dribbling and moaning like he's in pain, rocking and bobbing in the corner like a one-man boxing match. A head taller than Alice, but just as skinny. Same blond hair under his goofy orange hat, same blue eyes. Only his are totally spaced out.

Hogan stops and looks at me. "No one gets in," he turns to Alice, "or out."

"Fine," I say. "But how the hell are the police supposed to get in? Ever think of that?"

"Our plan right now," he says, "is to keep quiet. As long as that crazy guy out there doesn't know we're here, we're good."

Then the spazzy brother turns and, I kid you not, strips. He, like, totally pulls down his track pants and underwear—all the way to his ankles—and starts peeing in a urinal. Right in front of me.

"Ew." I turn away and cover my eyes. "Seriously?! Does he have to do that here?"

"It's a men's washroom, Izzy," Hogan says, like I don't already know. "Where else is he gonna go?"

The sound stops. But when I look back all I see is his hairy butt as he bends over to pull up his pants. "Ugh! Totally gross."

Click.

"Oh, come on, Xander!" I turn towards him still sitting on the floor. "Why? WHY?"

"Dude," Hogan shakes his head. "It's a butt."

"No," Xander corrects him, "it's a wide-angle candid of you all discussing his butt."

"This!" I gesture at him with both hands. "THIS is the kind of insane crap he was giving me for the yearbook. Can you believe it?"

"I already told you." Xander shrugs. "I don't choose. I just shoot. The Tank sees what it sees. It doesn't lie."

"Who is Tank?" Hogan asks.

"His dumb camera!" I say, rolling my eyes for emphasis. How idiotic. I mean, who names a camera? Even if you have no friends.

Think about it, loser. Maybe that's why you don't.

HOGAN

t's not that weird. I mean, lots of musicians name their guitars, like B.B. King had Lucille and Jimi Hendrix had Betty Jean. So he calls his camera the Tank. Dumb name, if you ask me. But I'm guessing he's never known a girl well enough to name it after.

"Alice! You're bleeding!" Izzy points at Alice's bare leg. Below her shorts there are red streaks from the back of her calf down into her sock.

Alice lifts her foot up on the sink and twists awkwardly to get a better look. Blood drips in splatters on the floor.

"Totally. Gross," Izzy says, leaning in like she's gonna help. But instead, she backs away and flaps her hands like Noah. "Ew! Ew! There's something in it! I can't even . . ."

Alice looks at me, her big eyes asking, and before I know it I say, "Want me to check?"

She nods, thankful.

I lean in. See a glint in the gash. "Yeah . . . looks like there's a piece of glass in it."

Alice unzips her fanny pack and pulls out a few Kleenex. "Can you get it?"

I look at her other three options. Izzy grossed out. Noah spaced out. And Xander zooming in and out.

"I'll try." I hold her leg steady in my left hand and pinch at the corner of the glass. It takes a few tries with my thick, stupid fingers. "I think I got it." The shard slides free easily enough, but the cut is pretty deep. I step on the sink pedal and turn on the taps. "Can you move closer to the water?"

She stumbles a bit, and I catch her with my arm, wrap it around to steady her as we try to rinse off her leg the best we can. Izzy continues her ew-ew-ew chant behind me, and Noah starts to play in the spray. He strums the streams like guitar strings until I lift my foot off the pedal and the spray stops. But he's still rocking to whatever water song keeps playing in his head. I wonder what it sounds like.

Alice hands me the Kleenex and I wad it over the cut. Already the white tissue is blood red. "It might need stitches. Got any Band-Aids in that fanny pack?"

She shakes her head.

On the floor, Xander unzips his backpack and hands me up a roll of gray duct tape. "Will this work? Duct tape is used by NASA. The Apollo 17 crew used it to repair their lunar rover when—"

"Yeah, okay," I snag it from him. "Thanks, Spock."

He frowns. "I just wasn't sure if you were familiar with the many uses of duct tape."

I rip a strip and press it to my fur a few times before sticking it over the tissue and around her thin leg. "My football initiation involved duct tape—I'm more than familiar with this stuff. Probably still missing a few layers of skin. Hopefully, this one won't stick as bad." I press around the edges. "It's not pretty, but it oughta hold for now."

"Oh, it will hold," Xander continues. "MythBusters were able to suspend a car and build a functional cannon out of duct tape. They even made a sailboat, canoe, and . . ."

Alice lowers her foot as Xander rambles on. I turn on the taps again, this time to rinse the blood off my hands. But as the water rushes over my fingers, I don't hear Xander's babbling or Noah's moaning, just a whooshing in my ears as red pools and swirls around the drain. Circling down, down, as the panic rises.

Stop.

Stop!

Stop the bleeding!

Alice puts her hand on my arm for a second. "Thanks." Her touch, her voice brings me back to the present, and I look at her. Embarrassed, she lets go.

"It could be worse," Alice says. "I bet there are a few kids right now who wish they were locked down in a bathroom instead of a classroom. At least we have toilets . . ."

Izzy folds her arms. "Rrrright. I am NOT using those."

". . . and a sink with water," Alice continues as I dry my hands.

Izzy sneers. "Definitely NOT drinking from that!"

"Well, if we were in Ms. Carter's class," Alice jokes, "we'd probably have to pee in the garbage can."

"Actually, it would be blue bin for liquids," Xander states, like it's clearly the obvious choice, "black bin for solids."

We all stop and stare at him. The guy is totally serious.

"You know," he explains, like there's a logic to it, "because feces are biodegradable."

"You are, like, SO disgusting," Izzy says. "Seriously. Don't even talk to me."

He shrugs. Takes a notebook and pencil out of his backpack and starts writing. I glance at the page. Sure enough, he's written his recycling plan.

"Why are you writing that down?" I ask, like there's a hope in hell he's gonna have a good explanation.

He looks up and blinks. "I am recording it for the autopsy." Then he goes back to his book.

And people think I'm crazy.

XANDER

Writer's Craft Journal

Xander Watt

March 11, 2016

REFLECTION: Of the writing genres studied so far, which one most appeals to you?

Social Autopsies. You may not be familiar with this genre. We don't learn them in Writer's Craft. But maybe we should. I first learned about them in grade 9.

You may not have noticed, but I have a hard time fitting in. It was worse in grade 9. Back then, I had a lot of meltdowns. But then Mrs. O'Neill in the Resource Room taught me how to write a Social Autopsy.

It's a dissection (just like a real autopsy), only this one does a postmortem on a conversation.

Conversation Facts
1. What is said often is not what is heard.
2. What is said often is not even what is meant.
3. People lie. A lot.
4. Even if they ask for the truth, most people don't want to hear it.

No wonder conversations leave me so confused.

Mrs. O'Neill also used photographs of facial expressions. For example, in Social Autopsy #27 she held up two photos and asked, "Was your teacher looking more like this or this when she said, 'Oh, sorry, Xander, am I boring you with this lesson?'"

I pointed to the expression most like Mrs. Brown's. Mrs. O'Neill said that usually when both eyebrows are up it is a "literal question." The person wants an answer. But that same question asked with one eyebrow up is a "rhetorical question." One you don't answer. Especially not with the truth. Especially not when it's, "Yes, actually, Mrs. Brown, this is the most boring lesson you've given to date. And you've done a lot of really bad ones."

Mrs. O'Neill told me that Mrs. Brown was being sarcastic.

sarcastic
/saˈkæstɪk/
adjective. using irony to mock or convey contempt. Snide. Scornful. Smart-alecky.

I wonder why it's okay for Mrs. Brown to speak sarcastically, but it's not okay for me to speak the truth? Either way, that Social Autopsy taught me a few things:

Observations
1. Don't yawn loudly in class. Even if you are bored or tired.
2. Don't give feedback unless asked. Even if it's something amazing that you think everyone should know.
3. If a teacher asks for feedback, 9 times out of 10, it's probably a trick.

Conclusion
Seek clarification. Ask, just to be sure. Always.

Social Autopsies help me make sense of the illogical, things like Mrs. Brown's moods, or group work, or even girls. I'm still dissecting that one—trying to crack the code. But Mrs. O'Neill tells me that even boys with the highest communication skills do not understand girls most of the time.

If that's true, then there's no chance I ever will.

Then Mrs. O'Neill asked me if I enjoyed our conversations, and I said yes.

"Well, I'm a girl," she continued. "So, what does that tell you?"

I thought about that for a minute.

Observations:
1. Technically she is a female. Even if her hair is cut like my bus driver, Pete's.
2. My mom is female. I like speaking to her.

Conclusion
I am quite comfortable speaking to middle-aged, overweight women.

But when I shared that insight with Mrs. O'Neill, something in her face made me think I should have asked for clarification first.

I do Social Autopsies on my own now. I even started collecting photos of sample expressions. Like the "you're annoying" face. I get that one a lot. I know that one now without even looking at my face charts.

I'm more skilled with the Tank and more invisible. I have collected a wide range of expressions. But I don't ask the subject for explanations (that usually leads to further Social Autopsies). Instead I take my photos to my grandfather at Pinehill Nursing Home. Grandpa Alex has Alzheimer's and doesn't remember me or our conversations, but he does know how to analyze expressions pretty well. I show him a picture and he defines the emotion: greed, joy, regret.

A group photo: "Angry mouth. Sad eyes. See how he's looking at the other guy who is talking to that pretty girl? Jealousy if I ever saw it."

A woman at the dinner table staring into space: "Tired. Sad, but bitter. Maybe vengeful. I'd say that poor girl got her heart broke."

He knew all that, even if he never recognized his own daughter in the picture.

So, of all the genres, I most like Comics . . . but I most need Social Autopsies.

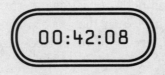

HOGAN

"**I**'m surROOUNded by EEEdiots," Noah mutters, eyes up on the ceiling. "Surrounded by EEEEEdiots."

I didn't think he could speak. I mean, just the way he acts. I didn't think he knew how.

"Did he just call me an idiot?" Izzy says, offended.

"No. It's Scar," Alice says. "From *Lion King*. It's his favorite movie. We've seen it a million times."

The way she says it makes me think she's not exaggerating.

The alarm sounds on Noah's watch and he heads for the door.

"No, Noah," Alice says, "we have to stay here."

Ignoring her, he yanks on the handle and, of course, being wedged shut, the door doesn't budge. He pulls harder, moans long and loud. His hands start flapping open and closed as he bobs back and forth, like that's gonna open it.

She looks at me apologetically as she tries to calm him down.

"It's just . . . well, he knows it's library time. This is when he shelves the books."

She grabs his hand and leads him to the corner by the towel dispenser. I think he's going to freak again. Run at the door or who knows what. Instead, he starts cranking out paper towel. Working the handle around and around, yelling out and clapping as the brown paper piles up on the floor.

Izzy looks at me. "How long do you think this will take?"

I like that she thinks I know. I wish I did. "No word from Bri?"

"No. Not about that. She's too busy bragging about all the fun she had at Kate's party last weekend."

"Kate Howard?" Alice asks, over her shoulder.

"Seriously? Don't tell me you were there!" Izzy looks at Alice in shock. "I mean, no offense but—"

"No. We're just neighbors." Alice cuts her off before the offense happens. Smart girl. "Gran had to call the police that night. The bonfire got way out of hand. It wasn't safe." She blushes then. Busies herself with cleaning up the paper towel. Probably feels stupid that she just ratted out her Gran.

Alice perks up. "Shh! Do you hear that?"

All I can hear is the squeak of Noah's cranking. But then I hear it too. Metal on metal. A slithery kinda clinking not far away. We freeze in silence, watching each other glance at the door. Finally it stops. And all is quiet again. Even Noah.

Alice whispers. "It sounds like—"

"Chains," I say.

"Chains?" Izzy goes. "For what?"

Is it part of his stupid prank—locking in everyone who is on a lockdown? I keep my mouth shut. There's no point in freaking them out even more.

Alice piles the paper towel in a heap on its rusted box as Noah starts pacing the small room. He drags two fingers along the brick wall like a car on a racetrack.

"There has to be a logical resolution to all this," Alice explains as she sits down beside me.

"This isn't a movie, Alice," Izzy argues, gathering a few of her scattered flyers to cover a spot on the floor. She settles herself on them, like they're a yoga mat. She crosses her tanned legs, careful not to touch the tiles. "This is real life. Not everything has a story."

Alice smiles. "But every person does."

I guess she's right. We all have one—even if it's one we'd rather forget.

"Think about it," she continues. "Whoever this guy is, he has a plot."

"You mean like a plan?" I ask.

"Exactly!" Alice nods, excitedly. "It's like The Hero's Journey, remember, Isabelle? Ms. Carter taught us that last week."

Izzy looks at her, confused. I guess she missed that lesson.

"Every hero reaches that point of no return," Alice explains. "And once he acts, once he crosses that threshold—everything changes."

I know all about that. Hell, I've spent the past two years regretting the moment I hit that point. The moment I hit my brother.

Maybe she is on to something.

"Wait, wait," Izzy interrupts. "Yeah, I remember now. But that's for heroes. Like Luke Skywalker, or Katniss, or Frodo. This guy, this psycho, whoever he is—he's no hero."

"Well, not in our stories, no," Alice agrees. "But he's probably a hero in his."

Ya, Hulkster. Just like how you're a real hero.

We sit in silence for a moment. Noah walks around the room tracing his finger through the grooves between the dingy bricks. He comes to the edge of the next brick, stops for a second, then changes direction. Up. Stop. Forward. Stop. Like he is finding a pattern in the chaos even if he is literally going in circles.

I think about what Alice said. It kinda makes sense. "So, what?"

"So," Alice rolls her eyes like it is so obvious, "if we knew a bit more about him, we could probably predict the ending."

Xander nods. "The Resolution."

Alice counts the possibilities on her fingers. "If he was bullied, he'd want revenge. Or if he was feeling insignificant—maybe this is his way of making his mark, like you said earlier, Hogan." She smiles at me.

I said that?

Yeah, I guess I did. I might not know the stuff teachers want, like this journey thing, but I do know what it feels like to be a nothing. A nobody. I know all about that. I can tell you what it feels like to grow up in someone else's shadow. And with all the things Randy did so well, that shadow was huge. It sucked to feel invisible when Randy was alive. But it's nothing compared to living in the total darkness of a dead brother's shadow.

Alice counts off her third finger. "Or he's just pulling a prank." Her pinky. "Or maybe he had a test and he didn't want to write it."

Or maybe he's a psychopath on a rampage. I don't say that one out loud.

Izzy pouts. "Well, even if we knew anything about this guy—which we don't—what good would it do?"

"Unless . . ." I say, as the idea clicks on like a bare bulb, "unless you know his fatal flaw."

Silence.

I look up to see all of them staring at me in surprise.

"What?" I shift, suddenly uncomfortable. "I read *Hamlet* in Dunne's class. And I didn't even read the play, okay? It was the graphic novel or whatever." I cross my arms.

Yeah, I listen in class sometimes. So what? I've skipped her class more times than I've sat through it.

Alice grins at me and I feel my scowl coming on.

"No," she says, "you're on to something."

I realize she's not laughing at me. I see it in her eyes. Something

I haven't seen from anyone in a long time. Something I thought I'd never see again.

Respect.

She looks back at the floor and taps her lip, deep in thought. "Every tragic hero does have a fatal flaw. A trait that brings him down."

"Ya," Izzy cuts in. "How about crazy? Lunatic? Demented? Oh, what does it matter, anyway?" Izzy moans in her melodramatic way. "We don't even know who he is."

They're both right. It is a hero's journey. And it is real life. But I hope to God I'm wrong. Because I learned something else in Dunne's class, something I am not about to share.

In a Shakespearian tragedy—everyone dies.

NOAH

Roundandroundandroundandround
      Paper towel rolling,
         rippling
            brown paper
               puddles on white tiles.

Out!
—the paper needs out!
Roundandroundandroundand—
               DONE!

Hummmmmmmm.

Stepping tile to tile.
Follow the rhythm of gray grooves

left
      and right
and left
      and right
and left—

Flap-and-flutter-and-flap-and-flutter-and—

Kim? I don't need to pee right now.
Out. I want out!

HummmmMMMm!

Finger follows cold grooves.
Where does it go?
How does it go?
Up. Stop.
   Across. Stop.
Down. Stop.
Stop and go. And stop. And go.
Around and around.

HummmmMMMmMMMMmmMmmMMmmmmM!
Never getting out. Never getting out!

Trapped inside a cement song.

ALICE

After a few laps around the room, Noah seems quieter. Well, quiet for Noah. This isn't where he is supposed to be, but he's walked the room, he knows the place. He's okay. For now. His "stimming," as the doctors call it, has slowed—almost no slapping or hand flapping, no bobbing and waving. He settles himself next to the Hulk and starts fiddling with the costume fur.

"You okay with that?" I ask, unsure, as Noah hums and rakes his fingers up and down through the Hulk's furry forearm.

It might turn into another "incident," one of those awkward moments that usually ended up with Kim re-teaching Noah from her Social Stories binder. Tales about Touchy Tom who didn't know about appropriate touching. Or Snot Scott who picked his nose. Or Naked Ned who took his clothes off in public places. Those story pictograms worked, funnily enough. They made sense to Noah. At least, we thought so. And it has been some time since he's done any of those unacceptable things.

But that doesn't mean he won't.

The Hulk shrugs. "As long as it keeps him quiet . . . and he keeps to just the arm—yeah. It's fine." He closes his eyes and rests his head against the wall. "Actually, it's kinda relaxing."

Noah hums as he strokes, his hoarse voice low and raspy like the lazy drone of a bumblebee.

"So, like . . . what's wrong with your brother?" Isabelle asks.

I hate that question—the assumption that he is "wrong." I know she doesn't mean it maliciously, but still.

"Geez, Izzy," the Hulk scoffs. "There's nothing wrong with him."

"Well . . . I know that." She blushes, unsure of how to proceed. "But he's High Needs, isn't he? I mean, look at him. The way he acts. The hat and everything. Come on, guys. It's not . . . normal, right?"

Noah's hum becomes a moan, but he keeps petting the Hulk's arm.

"Who knows what normal is?" the Hulk says before I can answer. He opens one eye and glances at me. "Does he normally do this?"

"Yeah." I smile. "Every day after school. He pets all our dogs in the kennel. It's a great calmer—for everyone."

"Makes sense." Leaving his arm in Noah's grasp, the Hulk stretches out on his back in front of Isabelle. "Izzy, you look real tense. Why don't you get started on my belly?"

She shoves him away with her foot. "In your dreams." He laughs and sits back up.

Izzy picks up the mascot head and fiddles with the remaining whiskers. "Just so you know, I wasn't asking to be mean. I just . . . I don't really know anyone who is . . . who acts like that." She looks at me, curious. "What's it like to have a brother like him?"

"I dunno, really." I shrug, unsure of how to answer. "I've never had any other kind of brother. That's just Noah. And he's not retarded." Not that anyone should be called that. "He is autistic."

"Can he be cured?" she asks.

A fair enough question, I guess. One of many I asked Gran growing up. Why does Noah still drool and have tantrums and poop accidents like a baby? What if I catch "oddism"? Why can't he do the things I can? Even then, I felt sorry for him and guilty about what I could do and he could not. In my dreams, Noah looks at me, laughs with me, speaks to me. In my dreams, he watches over me like a typical big brother. And when his night howling wakes me once again, because he usually only sleeps for two or three hours, I miss that brother in my dreams. I wish for him. Desperately.

"Gran showed me a documentary about autism," I continue. "Mozart, Einstein, Hans Christian Andersen, Isaac Newton, they probably would have been diagnosed on the autism spectrum. Autism isn't a virus or a disease, it's a way of being and seeing." I look at Noah. "It's how he is. A part of who he is."

I always wonder what the world looks like through his eyes, sounds like to his ears, or how it feels through his fingers.

"So, he's never gonna get . . . better?" she asks.

I asked that question too. So I give Isabelle the same answer Gran told me. "Well, he is learning better ways to communicate. But even if science ever discovers how to separate autism from the person, who you'd be left with would not be the same person you started with." As much as I wish for the brother in my dreams, I love the brother in my life.

Noah's fingers stroke up the Hulk's arm and into his hair, raking through the blond spikes.

"Woah!" the Hulk jerks away, frowning. "Personal space, man!"

My body tenses—ready to intervene, to explain, to protect.

But the Hulk simply takes Noah's hand and puts it back on the sleeve of his costume. "Stick to the arm, okay?"

I exhale, surprised to realize that I've been holding my breath.

Isabelle watches them, intrigued. And I am suddenly curious about her story.

What is her normal?

I bet she doesn't have to lock up her special things so they don't get broken or go missing. I bet she gets to sleep in. And take vacations. And eat in restaurants without people staring. I bet she can watch whatever she wants on television without having to deal with tantrums for *Lion King*.

"What's it like to be an only child?" I ask.

"I dunno." She looks down, shrugs one shoulder. "Lonely."

Click.

ISABELLE

Lonely. I can't believe I said that.

"Well, not . . . lonely," I add, "like, pathetic-loser lonely. Just . . . alone."

No one says anything. They just look at me . . . differently.

Is that . . . are they . . . like . . . feeling sorry for me?

"My dad and I are close," I add, and we are. "He travels a lot for work, though, so it's mostly me and my mother at home."

"Aren't you close with her?" Alice asks.

Too close. The woman smothers me. "No. I'd rather be alone in my room than sit through another one of her lectures about my weight, about my grades, about my messy room. Ugh. Nothing I ever do is good enough for her. 'Pizza? Oh, Isabelle. You know that gives you pimples!' 'I hear Jenny's daughter got early acceptance. Isabelle, are you sure you filled out the application correctly?'

"'Yes, Mother, I filled out the application correctly. You should know. You, like, made me go over it a million times.' She even came with me on the campus tour, which was just for students, and made the guide stop at the admissions office so my mother could double-check they got my application. Who does that, I ask you?"

"Your mother," Xander says.

"Thank you, Captain Obvious," I snap.

"You're welcome," he adds. "I've been working on my listening skills lately."

Awkward pause he doesn't hear.

"Maybe your mom is just trying to be helpful," Alice says.

"I don't need her help!" I blurt. "She still e-mails my teachers if my marks aren't 'fair' and then calls the principal if the teachers won't listen. She even called the soccer coach when I got cut at tryouts. Next thing I know, I'm back on the team, and my mother is volunteering as the new team manager."

"You got cut?" Hogan says, like it's ridiculous. It was, really. I am a totally better player than Kelly Cooper. Clearly, they made a mistake. Right?

"Your mom sounds kind of like a helicopter parent," Alice adds. "We learned about that in Anthro last semester. They like to hover over their kids."

"A helicopter?" I snort. "My mother is a full-on aerial assault."

"Man," Hogan says, "you must be just itching to graduate and move out."

I don't want to tell him I'm not, actually. For some reason, the thought terrifies me even more than being stuck at home.

"Where are you going, anyway?" he asks.

My phone vibrates and I look down, glad to have an out from this totally awkward conversation. I drop the mascot head and scroll through. There's a text from Bri telling me there are even more cops arriving—but still no word on who this guy is. A few Instagram alerts. And an e-mail. From Queen's University.

Oh. My. God. This is it.

I open it.

Pleasegodpleasegodpleasegod—

Two words in and my heart sinks: "We regret . . ." I don't have to read the rest to know what it says. It doesn't matter what it says. Nothing matters now.

I didn't get in.

XANDER

Given my photography skills, Mrs. O'Neill thought Yearbook would be the perfect course for my first semester. Isabelle Parks, the editor, did smile a lot at first. I thought I was cracking more of the girl-code. But as I handed in my assignments, I noticed she seemed to have "annoyed" face, even sliding into "WTF" range.

I talked to Mr. Strickland, the Yearbook teacher. And he told me there are "candid photos," where the person doesn't know you're watching. And then there are "stalker photos," where they don't want anyone watching.

Note to self: Photographing students = creeper.
Photographing celebrities = paparazzi.

So, I asked Isabelle for clarification, and Isabelle said: "Consider your audience. High school kids want to see pictures of themselves. Take shots of kids doing what kids do at St. F.X. Like basketball games or clubs or kids socializing. That kind of thing."

So I did. For the next three months, I took hundreds of pictures all over the school. I never went anywhere without the Tank. At sporting events. In the lunchroom. In the classrooms, the lab, the yearbook room. I took pictures of kids doing what kids do at high school—just like Isabelle Parks asked.

I spent hours in the darkroom developing negatives. I made her prints, four-by-six, in black-and-white, like she asked. But when I gave her the pictures, she freaked out. Like at the far, far end of freak-out: the "ohmigod he just ran over my dog" face.

Yes. She was that upset.

The next day, I got called to the principal's office to talk to Officer Scott, and to the guidance office, and did several autopsies with Mrs. O'Neill. But even after all that, I'm still confused.

Facts
* The pictures were well developed—no graininess or bubbles.
* Full tonal range. Check.
* Leading lines. Check.
* Good use of negative and positive space and light and shadow. Check.
* Rule of thirds. Check.
* Short depth of field. Check.

Conclusion
* Each photograph had excellent composition and layout.
* Every one told a story. At least a thousand words.

Hypothesis
Mr. Reeves would have given me an A+ on those in Photography class last year. I'm sure of it.

Facts
- I wasn't doing drugs or bullying or taunting.
- I wasn't having a meltdown in the High Needs hall or sulking on the team bench.
- I wasn't cutting or kicking or vandalizing or any of the hundreds of things the Tank caught kids doing.

Follow-up Question
So why, exactly, am I the one in trouble?

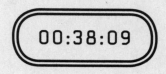

ALICE

sabelle sits consumed once again by her phone. But this time, she seems awkward. Almost embarrassed. Maybe even sad. Clearly, the perfect world of Isabelle Parks isn't so perfect.

"What the—?!" She brings the phone closer then drops it. It clatters against the tiles but Isabelle doesn't even notice. Instead, she just hugs her knees, drops her head on her arms, and rocks.

Is she . . . crying?

I look at the Hulk and he shrugs, just as confused.

"Isabelle?" I tentatively touch her arm. "Umm . . . are you okay?"

She shudders. Definitely crying.

"I'm sorry if I upset you," I say. "I mean, your mom probably isn't really a helicopter parent . . ."

The Hulk picks up her phone, glances at it, and turns it towards me. A photo. I recognize some kids from our school partying, red plastic cups raised as they cheer on a couple who are literally all over each other. The guy is Darren Greene. And he has her up against the doorframe, one hand pulling up her skirt, the other hiking up her leg while she runs her fingers through his hair. Hulk scrolls down the Instagram account and the photos get worse.

No wonder she's embarrassed. I'm embarrassed just looking at them.

"Don't worry, Izzy." He puts the phone down. "By next weekend, there'll be another party. Someone else will do something crazy and these pictures of you guys will be old news."

I don't bother reminding them that although these kinds of pictures might be forgotten, they will never disappear. Imagine her parents seeing that? Or her future boss? Like Officer Scott told us, there are dozens of scenarios where inappropriate photos can be problematic.

"Anyway," I add, trying to be somewhat optimistic, "you can't really see your face."

"It's not me," she says, her voice muffled in her arms.

"Well, alcohol changes people," I admit. "It makes you do crazy things. Like this one time? Gran was gone and I thought I'd try her crème de menthe. Just a taste. Next thing I know—"

"NO!" Izzy slams the floor with both hands. "Don't you get it? I wasn't there! I didn't go to the party!" Her scream bounces off the tiles in piercing echoes. Noah covers his ears with his fists. "The girl. With my boyfriend. Whoever she is . . . she's NOT me!"

She drops her head into her arms again and sobs.

Click.

I don't know what to say. Clearly, this is way worse than my minty barf-o-rama. Worse, even, than having Gran wake me at 6:00 a.m. to clean it all up. I still can't smell mint without gagging. I even have to brush my teeth with kids' Grapelicious.

"It's gonna be okay," I promise Isabelle with more confidence than I feel. Everyone knowing your boyfriend cheated—everyone but you—how do you clean up a mess like this? Especially when it keeps spilling from one person's phone to another.

Click.

". . . And Xander is gonna to delete all these pictures from today, right?" the Hulk says, giving him the stare.

"Um . . . no," Xander says in his monotone voice. "No. I cannot do that."

"What? Oh, yes you can—" the Hulk swipes for the camera but Xander is too quick.

"It's not possible!" Xander recoils into the corner, his camera clutched to his chest. "They cannot be deleted."

"Stop!" I shout, getting their attention and surprising myself. But they aren't listening—and they've totally forgotten all about Isabelle. Sighing, I look at Xander. "Why can't you delete them?"

"It's 35mm Ilford," he says, like that explains everything.

"Film?" I say. "You mean, it's not a digital camera?"

He nods, still breathless from the assault.

The Hulk scowls and sits back against the wall. "Whatever. Just get rid of them, loser. People should just mind their own business. Taking stupid pictures is what started all this mess." He looks at Isabelle. "It's probably just a dare. A stupid drinking game. And someone thought it would be funny to take a picture of it."

"It's not just that," Isabelle moans. "It's . . ." She sniffs and shudders. "I'm, like, killing myself to make this the perfect prom. Why bother? Darren's probably going with her, whoever she is. And how am I going to tell my parents that I didn't get into Queen's Commerce? The first Parks in five generations. Way to disappoint the entire family! Ohmigod, my mother is going to kill me!"

I want to tell her there's still a chance. Still time to raise her average in summer school or something. But her rant rages on.

"I can't believe I didn't get in." She pauses. "But what does it matter? Why should it matter? I don't even want to go there."

The photo of Darren, it seems, was the last straw. The final failure that pushed her over the edge, and now it all comes gushing out. And boy, can Isabelle gush.

"I'm trying!" she shouts, her head still in her arms. "I'm doing my best. But I can't do it all. I'm not perfect. And instead of hearing me, my mother is all 'sure you can, sweetie, we believe in you, you're a star, you can do it, we're behind you a hundred percent.'" Her body tenses with every word. The pressure coils in her small fists as she pounds her leg. "And it's push push push! If I make the team, they want me to be the MVP. If I run for Student Council, they tell me to go for President. My bulletin board is covered in gold stars and ribbons and honor certificates and medals. How many more do I need to win? How much more do I need to do before it's—" she hiccups and finally gasps for breath, "before I am enough?"

We sit in stunned silence, unsure if there is more to come. I look at the Hulk, who seems as speechless as me. I shake my head at Xander as he raises his camera and, surprisingly, he lowers it.

Somebody should say something. Do something. Unsure of what else to do, I pull a Kleenex from my fanny pack and put it in her hand. She pulls it under her curtain of hair to wipe her nose.

"It's not right," the Hulk finally says, "the way some Chinese parents push their kids like that."

Isabelle laughs then, a strange, sad echo in our room. "They're not Chinese."

The Hulk blushes. "I mean Japanese . . . or . . . whatever."

"No."

She lifts her head, revealing an Isabelle I've never seen before—one who is puffy-eyed and snotty-nosed. One who is broken. And real.

"I'm Chinese. They're white." She looks at the Hulk in surprise. "I'm adopted. I thought you knew that."

The Hulk looks away. Clearly he didn't know and feels bad about it. How would any of us know unless we'd met her family? Was it wrong to assume they were from the same culture?

"So," I continue, trying to understand what she is really saying, "your parents put a lot of pressure on you?"

"Yes." She hesitates. "Well, no, not exactly. I mean, they just expect it because I can. Because I should. Because I've been given so many opportunities." She says it like they aren't opportunities at all. Isabelle stares off beyond this tiny washroom. Beyond all of us. "I know it sounds ungrateful, but sometimes . . . sometimes I wonder what my life would have been like if they'd left me in that orphanage. If I wasn't . . . chosen."

Her voice hushes to barely a whisper. She isn't saying it to be heard or to impress us. And for the first time, I realize that Isabelle Parks' reputation as the "chosen one" isn't about us at all.

HOGAN

"Japanese . . . or . . . whatever"—who says that?

You did, moron.

I thought, I mean, I just assumed her parents were Asian too. I can say Asian. That's okay, right?

Nice, Hulkster. Add "racist idiot" to your loser list.

I know. I'm such an idiot. I'll bet she's never met anyone as stupid—

"Here's some good news," Xander blurts, cutting into my thoughts. He smiles at Izzy. I think he's trying to look encouraging or friendly—but it's just weird. Though not as weird as what he says next. "According to my observations, a quick Social Autopsy shows that you, in fact, have one less concern."

What is it with this guy and autopsies?

"I mean . . ." We all look at him and his face goes red. "Umm . . . Mrs. O'Neill says to focus on the positive. And, well, I'm 99.8 percent positive that you no longer have to worry about

Darren Greene." He smiles again, like he's come up with some great conclusion. "Because, clearly, he has replaced you with a different girl."

Izzy's mouth drops open.

Xander looks in confusion at each of us. "So . . . that's good . . . right? Because—"

I kick his foot and he shuts up. He raises his camera and retreats behind it.

Izzy's eyes fill up like two shot glasses.

"Don't even think about pressing that button," I snarl at Xander as he trains his lens on her. Is he for real?

"Whatever," Izzy says, wiping her nose. "I know I look bad now . . ." Like she could ever look bad. "But it's nothing compared to the other ones he took."

She pauses for second, then slowly pulls up her left sleeve. I think she's showing us some bracelet until I see the scars. Three of them. Red, angry slashes against the smooth skin of her inner arm. Like those lines people scratch on a cell wall. Counting down to freedom.

"Iz!" Without even thinking I reach out and squeeze her arm, like it just happened, as if by holding it tight I can take away some of the pain.

She avoids my eyes.

"Are they from an animal or something?" I say, knowing they aren't. "Bites or scratches from a dog?"

"Those are not from a dog," Alice adds, like I've offended her just by suggesting it. "A dog would never do that. Well, not any dog I've ever known."

I know she's right. The clean cuts. The short, straight lines. Those marks are intentional. A map of the dark places Izzy has been. But I want to give her an out. First the picture of Darren, and now this? It's too much.

"Well," I say to Alice, "not all dogs are as well trained as yours."

"It's not from a dog." Izzy looks up at Xander for a second. Then, breathing out, she lets it all go. "I was here late working on the yearbook, you know, trying to get it just right." Her voice is quiet. "The deadline was looming. And though I'd been accepted at a few other universities, Alyssa and Trev got early acceptances to Queen's Commerce, but I hadn't heard anything yet. And I started to wonder if maybe I wouldn't. And Darren was being weird. Cold. I could tell he was avoiding me. Things were getting worse. And my mother was constantly on my case. And I had this panic growing inside of me. A great big bubble of anxiety. What if the yearbook isn't good enough? What if everyone hates it? What if I don't get into Queen's? What if Darren doesn't love me any more? And the X-acto knife was on the desk and, I dunno. I just did it." She traced the lines with her finger. "It hurt. A lot. But it was . . . real. And it felt like . . ." She looks around like she's searching for the words. "Like I could finally breathe."

She stops and takes a deep breath again and her shoulders relax.

It's done now. Out. And even if she seems smaller somehow, deflated like an old balloon, I see in her eyes she's okay with it. Less tense.

"I know, it sounds crazy," she says. "Maybe I am. But I couldn't talk to anyone about it. Not even Brianne. No one could ever know." She looks back at Xander. "And then a few weeks later, he hands in his photos for the yearbook. A stack of black-and-white candids, stupid shots he took around the school. I hardly looked at the others, not when I saw the one of me." She stops. "And I saw it then, in that picture—I saw who I really was."

Izzy pulls both sleeves over her hands and draws up her knees, hugging them close as though she's trying to hold what's left of herself together.

Click.

"Sometimes," she says, "sometimes it's just really hard being me."

Alice opens her mouth to say something, but Izzy cuts her off.

"And don't tell me how great things are, because I know that. Or how great my life is—because I know that, too."

By the way Alice snaps her lips closed, I can tell that's exactly what she was going to say.

"But, see, when you guys make mistakes, it's okay." She looks at me, then—me, the King of Mistakes. "It's expected. Because, well, you're you."

I want to tell her it's hard for me, too. She has no idea what it's like to be me either. "Izzy, you're not the only—"

Alice's hand rests lightly on my arm and I stop. Look at her. Without even saying a word, she tells me to wait. Let Izzy speak. Just listen. I nod and Alice smiles. It's weird how we sorta read each other's mind. But cool weird.

Izzy keeps on talking. "MVP, Student Council President, leading actress, Yearbook Editor—and this year's book is the best one yet. I am successful at whatever I do. I'm not bragging. It's true. I've never failed. Ever."

"Must be nice," I mutter.

"It's not." Izzy rests her chin on her knees. "Failing is not an option. My mother wouldn't allow it. She does everything she can to prevent it. I keep trying to live up to that impossible standard. It's like, I keep clearing the bar, and they just keep on raising it. At some point it's all gotta come crashing down. The truth is . . ." her dark eyes fill with another shot of tears, "I'm not good enough. Not for Queen's Commerce. Not for Darren. And not for my mother."

No one speaks for a moment. What would we say?

"It's so funny, you know?" Izzy wipes her eyes with her ball of Kleenex. "I couldn't wait to grow up. But just the thought of leaving St. Francis Xavier, of graduating next month—it terrifies me." She swipes her cheek as another tear spills. "I know who I am here, what I can do. Where I fit in. But out there—in the real world—it's like . . . I will be nobody."

I look at Alice. Hope that she's got some wise words to say. She's smart, probably good with that kind of thing. But even Alice is silent. Just sitting there, staring at the floor deep in thought. Izzy looks at me then, like she's waiting for an answer. I look away. I've got nothing for her.

The truth is, she's just nervous, that's all. Izzy'll come out on top. She always does. She's just anxious about heading into the unknown.

But, me? I can't wait to leave this hellhole school where everyone is trying to help make me into something. I want to get away, to leave home, to get lost in that unknown where nobody knows about me or my brother.

Hell, I can't wait to finally be a nobody.

ISABELLE

BRI: They've got the footage from the atrium camera.

IZZY: Do they know who he is?

BRI: Not yet.
How you holding up?

IZZY: Worst. Day. Ever.

BRI: I know, right?

IZZY: I know about the party. About Darren.
Why didn't you tell me?

BRI: WHAT?!
Who told you?

IZZY: I saw the pictures on Kate's account.

BRI: OMG! Iz, I am SO SORRY.

IZZY: You should be. Why didn't you tell me? A best friend
would tell.

BRI: You're right. I should have. I just didn't know what to say.

IZZY: For a start . . . how about: your boyfriend is a lying ass.

BRI: I know. I know.

IZZY: What happened?

BRI: I dunno. He was drinking a lot and I guess things just got out of hand.
You know how he is.

IZZY: Ya.

BRI: And, like I said, you've been different lately.
He said things weren't going good between you.

IZZY: :(I know.

BRI: And next thing I know . . . we got carried away.

IZZY: Wait . . . WHAT?!
WE??!
That's YOU in the pictures?!

BRI: I thought you knew!
You just said you knew.

IZZY: I said HE cheated.
OMG! I didn't know it was with MY BEST FRIEND.
I can't believe you guys.
What the hell is wrong with you?

BRI: I'm so SO sorry.
Please believe me, Iz.
I never meant for that to happen.

IZZY: Don't EVER talk to me again.
I'm DONE.
With BOTH of you.

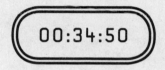

ALICE

We've been in lockdown for a good twenty-five minutes, though it feels so much longer. Surely there must be some kind of update. Things have gotten quiet since the last blasts, but they haven't let us out yet. Which must mean the shooter is still out there. Somewhere.

"Any news?" I ask Isabelle as she furiously texts.

"Yes! Get this, that girl in the picture?" She clenches her jaw. "It's Bri. As in, my-best-friend-Bri, all over my boyfriend." She slams the phone down on the floor. "She knew things weren't good between me and Darren lately—the perfect time for her to weasel in. They freaking deserve each other."

No one speaks.

"Isn't he going to play football for California State next year?" the Hulk finally asks.

"Long-distance relationships don't usually last," I add, like I know anything about dating that doesn't come from a novel or the old Turner Classic Movies Gran and I watch on Friday nights. "It might be for the best, Isabelle. Even if it doesn't look like that now."

"Duh!" She rolls her puffy, red eyes. "I KNOW that! I get it. We talked about breaking up after graduation—well, he talked about it. But in my heart I always hoped . . ." Her voice trails off.

I finish it for her. "That one day he'd wake up, change who he is, and realize how much he really loves you." It's a classic TCM plot—*The King and I*, *The Sound of Music*, all the greats have it.

Isabelle smiles wistfully. "Absence makes the heart grow fonder. That's what they say, right?"

"Not any guy I know," the Hulk mutters. "More like, what happens in Vegas stays in Vegas."

Clearly he needs to watch some better programming.

"I thought he'd wait until after prom." Isabelle chews her lip. "That he'd give me that, at least—after all I've done for him. But no!" She shakes her head. "He goes behind my back with my best friend and they make a fool out of me in front of the whole school."

"It's not the whole school," I correct her. I'm trying to help her keep things in perspective. "We didn't hear about it. Not everyone knows."

"Well, everyone that matters. No offense." And just like that, the old Isabelle is back. Making me keep things in perspective too.

HOGAN

"Not to be insensitive," Alice goes, "because I know you have a lot going on right now, but I just wondered . . . if Bri might have mentioned anything about the, um, lockdown?"

Izzy sighs, irritated by any drama outside of her own. "I dunno. I think the police are checking the atrium's security cameras."

"I didn't even know we had atrium cameras," Alice says, surprised.

"Me either," Xander mutters.

We sit in silence. Izzy notices a white paper among the yellow flyers on the floor. She picks it up and glances at it. "This e-mail has your name on it, Alice."

"Oh, I must have dropped it when I fell." Red-faced, Alice pratically snatches it from Izzy's hand, but not before Iz reads, "University of British Columbia? Bad news?"

"Something like that." Alice looks away as she crumples it.

"UBC Creative Writing Program?" Xander says. "I'm surprised you got a rejection. You are, by far, the most talented writer in Ms. Carter's class."

Alice fidgets like she doesn't know what to say or where to look. Her face glows bright red.

"Are you angry?" Xander asks. "Was I not supposed to say that?"

"No, you're right," Izzy says. "She's blushing because you pointed out something true. I might not have remembered your name at first, Alice, but I'll never forget your stories. Especially that one about the pirate queen. That was awesome."

"And the dog one," Xander goes. "Remember that?"

"Thanks, guys." A small smile pulls the corners of her mouth. "Actually it's . . . a letter of acceptance."

We all congratulate her, and her shy smile widens until her cheeks dimple. Even her eyes are glowing like she's lit up from the inside and not from the shaft of afternoon sunlight coming in through the small window up in the corner. Beside her, Noah waves his hand in front of his face, as if strumming the beams.

Alice rests her hand on his leg and he slows. Her smile fades. "But I'm not going."

"What?" Izzy's jaw drops. "That's, like, one of the top schools in the country. Seriously, that's huge, Alice. You HAVE to go!"

"I can't," she says, sadly. "I just . . . can't."

"It's because of Noah, isn't it?" I say, not totally getting how I knew. Just that I did.

She meets my eyes and nods.

"What about your parents?" Iz asks. "Can't they take care of him?"

"We live with my grandmother," Alice says. "And our mom . . . isn't around."

"Is she dead?" Xander blurts in his doofus way. Jerk.

"No," Alice says, "my mom left when I was about three and Noah was seven. Like, literally, left us with Gran and Grampa. People say their dogs are 'going to live on the farm' when they can't handle them any more. Apparently, my mom thought it was okay to do that with her kids." She stops for a second and chews her lip.

"At least you know who your mom is," Izzy says. "I'll never know my birth mother."

Leave it to Izzy to try and trump it with her story. Nothing supportive ever starts with the words "at least"—

At least Randy didn't suffer.

At least your parents have you.

At least you had a brother.

"I do know who my mother really is," Alice says. "That's part of the problem."

Noah hums like a wasp's nest. He's getting louder, winding up inside, or something. Alice finally lets go of his leg and he jumps up and starts pacing again.

"I get it, though," she continues. "A young single mom. Noah was in pretty bad shape then, too. Violent. Didn't communicate. Hard to manage. Leaving him at Gran and Grampa's farm was probably the best thing for him."

"But what about you?" Izzy asks.

Alice bites her lip again.

"See?" Xander goes. "Her face is red. You said something true."

"It doesn't matter what I want," Alice tries to explain. "Grampa left the farm to Gran—"

"So he's dead?" Xander cuts in again.

Izzy rolls her eyes.

"Yes. He died this past winter," Alice explains. "Gran said she couldn't keep the kennels and run the farm and take care of Noah all on her own. They only let him attend high school until he's twenty-one, so that means this is his last year here at St. F.X., too. So I told Gran, she isn't on her own. That I'm not going anywhere. That I'm not Mom." She shrugs. "Gran needs me. Noah needs me."

It's like I'm seeing her for the first time. Not the scrawny klutz that came tripping into the washroom. Not the blushing nerd who can't shut up. Just a girl who cares—a sibling who would do anything for her brother. No matter what the cost.

Maybe that's what siblings are supposed to be like.

"What about what you need, Alice?" Izzy's voice brings me back. But I know what Alice is going to say, even before I hear it.

"My needs don't really matter," she says. "It's always about Noah."

Like how it's always about Randy. Even now.

"Don't get me wrong, I don't always like it," Alice says. "But that's just the way things are."

And you can't change the way things are.

ALICE

The Hulk is watching me, but his expression is different, somehow. He gets it. He knows what I'm talking about.

But Isabelle clearly doesn't. "Sounds like you're a supporting character in your own life." She shakes her head, disgusted. "It's your life, Alice. You should be the lead."

I don't expect her to understand. "It is what it is."

"It's not fair!" Isabelle gives me that look—the one I see countless times from strangers whenever Noah stims or hums, freaks or flaps, or bobs or babbles—whenever he does the million things that make him Noah.

They look at me with pity.

I hate that the most. Pity doesn't do me any good, and I should know. I've wallowed in it many nights. Right around 4:00 a.m., when those questions I buried all day came bubbling back up:

Why?

Why did she leave me?

Why didn't she take me with her?

Why doesn't she call more often?

Why doesn't she love me?

Gran says Mom doesn't have the strength to deal with Noah. Or the guts to face the guilt. It's just easier for her to stay away. To keep busy. To forget.

The Hulk speaks, his voice strangely quiet. "Life's not fair."

"Not fay-yar," Noah echoes, in his Scar voice, "not fay-ar. Life's not fay-ar." He has the words and the British accent down. I wonder if he has any idea what it really means.

The Hulk continues, "But you can't run from it—no matter how hard it gets. Because if you start running—you just never stop." He looks at me, in me. He understands. "I don't know about missing moms, but I'd give up anything . . . anything to have my brother here."

And for the first time in my life, I see a look, not of pity, but of longing. The Hulk wants what we have, Noah and I.

I meet his eyes. Hold them for a moment. "Thanks . . . Hogan." He shrugs it off like it's no big deal. But it is, for me it's huge.

"Okay—but your brother is definitely dead," Xander blurts at Hogan. "That I know because—"

"Xander!" Isabelle cuts him off. "Geez, don't you have a filter?"

"No." Confused, he looks down at his camera. "I never use one. I'd rather see things as they really are."

We sit in awkward silence, looking everywhere but at each other.

"He's right. It's true." Hogan lets out a deep breath. "It's been two years, I should be able to at least say it."

But he doesn't.

Xander tilts his head and stares at Hogan. "But is it true that you killed him?"

I gasp. People gossip like that behind Hogan's back—but only Xander is dumb enough, or maybe honest enough, or brave enough to say it to his face.

Hulk Hogan killed his brother.
I heard he stabbed him in the change room.
No, he squashed his head like a melon—right between his palms.
Blood everywhere.

It can't be true, right? It has to be just a rumor. It's too terrifying, too unbelievable. Hogan stares at the splatters of red drops on the white tiles. Blood from my cut. Nobody moves, or speaks, or even breathes.

"I did it," he finally says, his voice barely a whisper. "I killed my brother."

HOGAN

Randy and me were raised to fight. Hell, my parents even named us after their WWE heroes Macho Man Randy Savage and Hulk Hogan. That was us. "The Mega Powers." He was two years older than me. Two years stronger. Two years smarter. And I hated it. Hated losing all the time.

No matter how I tried as a kid, Randy always won. Beating me, literally, with his chokeholds and atomic drops, his hair-pull hangman, and then, finally, jumping off our bunk beds in his signature finish: a diving elbow drop. "Ooooh yeah!"

"Randy!" Mom would yell from the kitchen. "Stop picking on your brother!"

He'd laugh then. And that only made it worse—that I needed my mom to save me.

"Had enough, Hulkster?" he'd tease with that stupid smirk. And, room spinning, I'd get up and go back for more, when really I should've stayed down.

I should have stayed down.

In grade 10, I made the St. F.X. football team—much to Randy's surprise. And I was good—much to mine. All that wrestling, all those years learning to deke Randy's grasp, learning to push back, I guess it paid off. In tryouts, I blew past the O-line and broke through the block. Before I knew it, I was diving for Randy. Body-slammed him before he had a chance to throw. I stood up over him, held out my hand. But he slapped it away.

Holy crap, it felt good.

"Nice hit, Hogan," Coach Dufour said, coming to stand beside me. He smacked my shoulder pad. "Looks like there's a new King in town."

Everyone laughed. Well, everyone but Randy.

Coach double-teamed me, made it even harder for me to get at Randy. But that made me push even more. Pretty soon, it got to the point where Coach pulled me aside. "You can ease up a bit when you break through the line. Just in practice. I can't have you breaking our quarterback."

I felt like my chest was going to burst. He might as well have shouted at me to "stop picking on your brother."

Everything changed then. People noticed me. Randy wasn't the KING. He was just R. KING now. I smiled when Mom sewed his new name patch on his game jersey, and even more when she sewed mine: H. KING. This was his last year on the team. But I was just getting started. Who knew how far I could go? Even Coach said that.

And at the home opener, I had this feeling their quarterback was gonna pass to the tight end, so I broke off the line and stuck with my man. My gut was right, and next thing I know, I'm catching an interception. An interception! I even ran it back the length of the field for the winning touchdown as Izzy and her friends jumped and cheered me on. For the first time, I felt like the Fabulous, the Incredible, the Amazing Hogan King. Hell, after I reached the end zone I even did

Hulk Hogan's signature move—cupped my hand to my ear to hear the crowd roar.

And did they ever.

I was a new man after that. I was someone people noticed and admired. I wasn't Randy's little brother; I was the Hulk. I could do anything. Maybe even get Izzy. Perfect, amazing Isabelle Parks. Because if I had her, then I'd have it all. And when she kissed me at the bonfire that night—I felt like that shooting star overhead. I thought it was a sign, that streak of light.

But I know now, it was what it was. A hunk of nothing, burning up and fizzling out as it fell.

"Nice game, loser," Randy said in the locker room after our defeat in game five. It was my fault. I'd played terribly. Whatever streak I'd been on early in the season had fizzled out. Their running back broke through my gap twice, and even the quarterback snuck around my end—all of them touchdowns. All of them my fault. Even the interception, the gift thrown right to me, hit me in the helmet and bobbled free.

He stood in his underwear, still dripping from his shower as he rubbed his hair with a towel. "Maybe football isn't your sport. Why don't you see if Isabelle wants you on her cheerleading team? No, wait, they won't want you doing the lifts." He laughed, and threw the wet towel at me. "You might fumble a cheerleader."

"The way he's playing," Darren Greene echoed, "fumbling might be the only thing he'll ever do with a cheerleader!"

The room exploded in jeering.

"You're right," I admitted, "their three TDs were on me. But our TDs . . . or lack of them," I turned to face Randy, "dude, that's on you."

His smile dropped.

I waved my arm at the team. "They can't catch . . . if you can't throw."

The room went silent. I'd broken some unwritten rule, I guess. Or maybe, maybe I'd hit the nail on the head. He'd been

125

off his game just the same as me. Only nobody called him on it. Nobody ever called Randy on anything.

I opened my locker to grab my shirt and I never saw him coming. My face hit the metal doors and he pummeled my side. I shoved back, hard. He staggered into his teammates, who had circled around, but they pushed him up, pushed him on. It was our WWE bedroom brawl all over again, only this time he had an audience and they were cheering his name.

Ran-DEE! Ran-DEE! Ran-DEE!

I was on their team too, but no one was cheering for me. I realized then how stupid I was to think I mattered. A lineman, like me, was expendable. A finger. One of many. But a quarterback, well, he was the heart of the team—and I'd stupidly just taken a stab at it.

I looked at them all chanting his name, eager to see me get my ass kicked.

Screw them! I turned my back. Screw them all!

"C'mon," Randy taunted. He shoved my shoulder. Once. Twice.

My fists balled.

"Let's go . . . Hulkster," he said, sarcastically. "Show us what you got."

He jumped me from behind. Slipped his palm up around my neck in a half nelson. And, just like that, he had me locked in, driving me to my knees. I felt it bubbling up inside me, that familiar rage. The one only Randy could stir up.

"Quit it!" I yelled, breaking free and shoving him hard. My chest heaved.

"Quit it!" he mimicked. "Or what? You gonna tell Mom?"

He smirked, that stupid smile I always hated. "Maybe I should give Isabelle a call. Show her what it's like to be with a real Macho Man." He thrust his hips in and out. "Oooooh yeah!"

I don't remember running at him or tackling him or even hitting the floor, next thing I knew we were punching, wrenching, kneeing—in a full-on, all-out brawl. Only we weren't kids goofing around on carpets and mattresses, we were almost five hundred pounds of muscle and madness.

Randy slammed my head into the floor, and I saw stars explode and fizzle. When I came to on my back, he was standing on the bench just over me, getting the crowd wild as he readied for his classic diving elbow drop. The one I'd seen a million times before.

Only this time . . . I struck first.

I kicked hard. Swept his legs out from under him. Randy fell back off the bench. Back into the lockers, slamming his head against the corner of the one I'd left open.

He dropped.

"Ooooouo!" the guys shouted. "Nice one, Hogan!"

But I didn't care what they thought. I didn't care about any of that as I crawled over to Randy. He hadn't moved. And Randy never stayed down.

"Randy?" I turned his face towards me. His eyes were open—but not seeing. A dark gash on the side of his head oozed red. It ran into a sticky puddle that spilled wider and wider with every second.

"Holy shit!" I shook him slightly. "Randy! Randy! Wake up!" I looked at the team, now silently gathered around us, the terror I felt mirrored and multiplied on their faces.

"Somebody!" I yelled. "Get help!"

I lifted Randy's head and pressed my palm over the wound. That's what you're supposed to do, right? Stop the bleeding? Stop the bleeding!

STOP THE BLEEDING! Please God, make it stop!

But the blood oozed hot and slick through my fingers; my brother's life, pooling red in the grooves of the gray-tiled floor as it ran to the drain.

ISABELLE

"It was an accident," I say, but Hogan won't even meet my eyes.

I know what he's thinking, the poor guy. That's why I have to convince him. I know how much Hogan idolized his brother, and how proud Randy was of him. I don't know exactly what happened that day in the change room. But whatever it was, I know it was a mistake. It had to be.

"Hogan. It wasn't your fault."

I tried to tell him that for months after the accident. But he wouldn't listen. Wouldn't even return my phone calls. It was like a part of him died when his brother did, and he shut everyone out. Even me.

I thought I mattered more than that.

Come to think of it, I've thought I mattered more to every guy I've fallen for. But I get it now. They all saw me as a trophy. A conquest. Another one of their awesome achievements: get Isabelle Parks.

Hogan, John, Trevor, and now Darren—the players who played me. Did Coach Dufour, like, make that a part of their spring training? Break records. Break the O-line. Break Isabelle's heart.

Each time, I thought it was my fault. That I'd done something wrong. Or that I hadn't been enough. Or gone far enough. And every time a guy shattered my world, Bri came over to patch it together with facials, chick flicks, and two tubs of Chocolate Peanut Butter Häagen-Dazs. When Hogan shut me out. When John dumped me (by text—seriously?!). When Trev and I went on-and-off-again for about four months. After that last messy breakup with Trev, I swore I'd never let any guy EVER hurt me like that again.

Little did I know, the next person to break my heart would be Bri.

The worst part of this whole mess isn't about Darren. Darren is Darren. A prick. And if I admit the truth to myself, maybe he was a bit of a trophy for me, too. I'd never dated a quarterback before. Honestly, our relationship was temporary, at best.

But Brianne. BRI?

How could she do that to me?

We'd been through so much together. Girl Guides. Training bras. Braces. Boyfriends. I was there for her through her parents' divorce, and all the times she needed a place to escape this past year when Social Services got involved. We were supposed to be each other's bridesmaids—friends for life. And yet, she threw it all away on a dare. If that's what it was. A stupid drunken fling.

Did I mean so little to her, too?

Alice catches my eye. She looks concerned. After my freak-out, I don't blame her. I feel like I'm having a heart attack, or a panic attack, or some kind of nervous breakdown.

My face is flushed, my head is pounding, and my heart literally aches. I take a few deep breaths and close my eyes. One meltdown today is enough. Mom keeps telling me these are "the best days of my life." Dear God, if things get any worse than this, I won't be able to take it.

I look at Alice's fanny pack. "Got any Tylenol in there?" I'm that desperate. I'd actually take whatever she had.

"Sorry." She shakes her head as she pulls out a roll of Life Savers and offers it to me. A green candy peeks from the tattered wrapping. Bits of tissue and dog hairs and god-knows-what-else are stuck to it.

Okay. Maybe I'm not that desperate. Besides, I usually only eat the red and orange ones.

Alice holds it out to me and smiles with her big eyes like some kind of demented Twisted Whiskers card. Like she's offering me her left lung. Like it would literally kill her if I said, Um . . . no thanks.

So I take the candy. Pop it in my mouth. Try not to gag. Ugh, the things I do for people.

"Look, Hogan," I say, determined to be heard. He ignored my phone calls and texts back then, but he can't ignore me now. "I know you must miss your brother. And I think you blame yourself for . . . for what happened."

He picks at his cuticles until they bleed. A habit, I guess, judging by the scabs on his other fingers. Just another way to vent a pressure cooker of pain. I know all about that.

"But you have to believe it wasn't your fault." I need him to get it.

"What do you know about it, Iz?" He doesn't look up. "You weren't there."

"No," I say. "But I know you guys were close. I know how much Randy cared about you."

Hogan lifts his eyes to mine. "Cared? Randy didn't give a crap about me."

"What?" I remember the way Randy used to look at Hogan with such pride. Heck, it was Randy who told me Hogan was interested in me. "Don't be ridiculous. He talked about you all the time."

"Ya," Hogan mutters, "trash-talked."

Ohmigod! Why is he being so hard-headed about this? "At least you had a brother. At least you had fifteen years together."

Hogan finally looks up, stares at me like what I'm saying isn't something good. "Yeah. AT LEAST."

"Seriously," I say, "I'd give anything to have a sibling."

Everyone thinks they'll be happy when they get the next iPhone or trip, or Kate Spade purse. But what if you had all of those things? What if you got whatever you wanted, whenever you wanted it—and you were still unhappy? What do you hope for then? On the DREX trip, I realized the people we met there had a richness to their families that I've never known. And when I came home and pulled back the curtain on my life and saw the real Oz—I saw the sad truth. All this time, I've just been kidding myself. My life is not happy. Or perfect. Or loving. It's empty.

I don't expect them to get it. Alice, Hogan, Xander. My life is just too complicated for them.

I look back at Hogan, willing him, at least, to understand about Randy.

"I partied with those guys a lot, Hogan. Probably more than you." He doesn't argue. We both know it's true. "And yeah, Randy trash-talked about a lot of guys, but never you. When it came to his big little brother, Hulk Hogan—Randy loved to brag."

HOGAN

"It wasn't your fault."

All kinds of people said that. The cops. Coach. The team. But it wasn't true. Because the people that mattered most—they didn't believe it. Not my mom. Not my dad. Not Randy. Not me.

Mom tried to comfort me. But how could she? How could she be kind to the kid who caused her so much pain? I heard her crying. Missing him. How could I let her hug me and pretend like things were okay? Like she didn't wish it was Randy in her arms—and not me.

Dad worked more at the office. Avoided his grief, and the cause of it, altogether.

And I . . . well, I don't know what I did really. These past thirty-one months, the 939 days since my brother died, they're all just one long blur.

I quit the team. Quit talking to Izzy. And, after a while, she quit calling. It was better that way. People were so uncomfortable around me. I felt their stares, heard them whisper as I walked past. I was famous now, finally famous. But for all the wrong reasons. Even the teachers seemed to tense just a little when I happened to come to class.

Why bother?

"It is what it is," Coach said one time when we straddled our bikes at the top of the Gatineau Hills, waiting for the rest of the class to catch up. "It's a damned tragedy. But punishing yourself for the rest of your life, well, Hogan," he looked off into the sky, "that'd be a tragedy too."

He never said anything more after that. Which was just as well. That one sentence gave me a lot to think about as I rode back home.

"When it came to his big little brother, Hulk Hogan—Randy loved to brag," Izzy says, trying so hard to convince me of something that isn't true. More than anything, I wish it were. But how could he be proud of the brother that put him in his grave?

I clench my jaw.

"Oh!" Xander says, like he's just put two and two together. "Hulk Hogan, the wrestler. I get it. Your name is Hogan. Yes, that makes sense now. All this time, I thought you were named after the Incredible Hulk."

We look at him.

"You know, Dr. Banner and the gamma rays?" Xander says, like we all speak geek. "It's a Marvel—"

"I know who he is," I snap.

"Of course you do. He's famous now." Xander rummages in his bag and pulls out the *Marvel Encyclopedia*. Flips to Incredible Hulk's page, even though I bet he's got the whole thing memorized. "He appeared in 1962, but for the first five issues the Incredible Hulk was not an immediate success. Probably because he is not typical hero material." He looks at me. "You know, you might be more like him than you think."

"Great," I say. "Thanks."

Xander continues, like anyone cares. "And—"

"This isn't the time for trivia," Alice interrupts. This from the queen of fun facts.

"But don't you get it?" he continues.

"What?" I ask, sure I'll be sorry I did.

"For years, he was just the sidekick in a bunch of other heroes' stories." Xander flips the page and holds up a two-page spread of the Hulk: torn purple shorts, bulging green arms, boulder-sized fists clenched overhead. A typical teeth-gnashing pose. "And . . ." Xander continues excitedly, like he's saving the best for last, "he's the symbol of subconscious rage."

Everyone looks at me like I'm going to explode.

I stare back. What's their problem? Why are they looking at me like that?

"What?" I say, defensively.

No one speaks.

Finally, Alice clears her throat. "Um . . . you do give off a bit of a . . . hostile vibe."

"Hostile vibe?" Izzy snorts. "That's one way to put it. Seriously? You've been an angry ass since Randy died." She pauses. "No offense."

That I can agree with. That I know to be true. I have felt nothing but anger or numbness since Randy died. Anger at him for pushing me. Anger at myself for taking the bait. Anger at my parents for loving him more. At him, for always being better. And especially, anger that he wasn't better that day in the change room, in our last match. Even when I win, with Randy, I always lose.

Oh yeah, Hulkster! When you gonna learn? You can never win against me.

"You're right—" The words snag in my throat and I say it louder. "You're all right. Even Xander . . . I've always felt like I played second best to my brother. Even after he died." I pause. "Probably more now."

No one says anything. In the corner, Noah hums.

Xander closes his book and puts it back in his bag. He seems proud of himself for sharing—even though he seems to have no idea what just happened here.

"But the Hulk did eventually get his own successful strip in 1968," he says, and smiles that weird smile. "And today, he's one of Marvel's key characters."

"Which goes to prove," Alice adds, directing her statement to Izzy, "that even a hero can play the role of supporting cast."

"Or," Izzy points out, pulling out her phone as it buzzes, "even a supporting character can become a hero herself."

Funny how people can see the exact same thing in so many different ways.

ISABELLE

BRI: I know you're not talking to me.

IZZY: I'm not.

BRI: I just thought you'd want to know they've identified the shooter.

IZZY: Fine. Just tell me.

BRI: Maxwell Steinberg.

IZZY: Who?

BRI: Exactly. I've never heard of the guy. But he goes to St. F.X.

IZZY: What grade?

BRI: Dunno. But they say he's the one who shot out the atrium displays and set off explosives in the stairwells.

IZZY: Where is he now. What's his plan?

BRI: That's the big question, isn't it?

IZZY: No, Bri.
I have MUCH bigger questions than that.

ALICE

axwell Steinberg." Isabelle looks up from her phone. "Anybody know him?"

Hogan and I shake our heads.

She glances at Xander's backpack by his leg. "Got a yearbook in there?"

He hesitates for a second, like he doesn't want her to see it, then he reaches in his bag and hands the book to her. It's navy, with the school's logo embossed in green on its cover, just like every other yearbook. Only on this one, the big X has been colored red and a red circle drawn around it.

Isabelle looks at it in disgust, clearly annoyed that someone had defaced her cover design. "Well, that's original." She flips open the cover revealing a blank page—just like mine. I guess he hasn't asked for signatures either. Because who's going to sign it? And what would they write, anyway?

Have a good summer, whatsyourname. It was nice NOT knowing you.

She skips over the grade 12 pages. "He's not grade 12, I know that. I had to edit all the grad write-ups." She glares at Xander, like it's his fault. "I know his name's not there."

"Not all grade 12s got grad pictures or did write-ups," Hogan says, defensively.

"Well, duh. But there's only five leftovers." Isabelle keeps flipping, oblivious to the way her casual dismissal of Hogan makes him grit his teeth. "Doddson, French, Garamond, you, and Styles. Steinberg's not a grade 12."

She stops at the grade 11 portrait pages and runs her finger down the Ss. "Stanley . . . Steele . . . Steepleson . . . Steinberg. Here. That's him."

We lean in over the page and examine the two-by-three black-and-white of some random kid. He's wearing a superhero T-shirt. Short brown hair. A few pimples. An awkward smile.

"Recognize him?" she asks.

I shake my head. I don't think I've ever seen him before. He's familiar in his averageness. He could be anybody—he looks like everybody. Which, ironically, makes him a nobody.

"If he was on a team or a club or anything noteworthy in the yearbook, I'd probably know about him," Isabelle says.

"Noteworthy or not," I add, "if this guy goes to our school and is under the radar, only someone really watching would notice him."

Xander isn't looking at the picture. But if anyone saw this guy, it would be him.

"Xander," I ask, "have you ever taken photographs of this guy?"

Isabelle turns the page towards him. He looks at it, blinks a few times, and then pulls a Nike shoebox from his backpack. The cardboard is worn and frayed at the edges. The end label reads: "Cross-Trainers: Size 5 Boys." He sets it on his lap and lifts the orange lid. Inside are photos—hundreds of four-by-six black-and-whites. He dumps the box on the tile floor and spreads them around, searching through their glossy rectangles for the one he has in mind.

I pick up a picture.

In it, a teacher, back to us, looms over a student sitting at a desk. The kid, facing the camera, is cringing, clearly on the hook for something.

Xander glances at it as he rummages. "Shame—that's shame. It's kind of like guilt." He picks up another and hands it to me.

In the second shot, taken through the back door windows, a wide-eyed kid stands, mouth agape. You don't have to see the smashed glass or the slingshot in his hand to know what he's done.

"Sometimes they're hard to tell apart," he says. "Like . . . uh . . . this one." He hands me another.

This one shows the chairs outside the VP's closed door where two kids sit, their clothes ripped, lips bloodied. One holds a baggie of ice to his forehead.

"This face is shame—sad, sorry, regretful," Xander says, pointing to the guy with the ice. "He obviously did something, probably started the fight. And he's been given his punishment. But this guy." He points at the other one, staring at the door. "See the way he's worried? But still angry, like, how his chin juts out? That's guilt. He knows what he did was wrong, but he doesn't know what is going to happen yet. I bet there's a third guy in there ratting him out."

The puddle of pictures spreads as he rummages. Each one a crucial moment captured—a whole story, really, contained in four by six inches.

A close up of Mr. Jinder picking his nose as he marks assignments at his desk.

Some girl cheating off her neighbor's test.

Some freckle-faced guy jeering and pointing.

Mrs. Tripp lighting up a cigarette in her car.

A scrawny basketball player slumped alone on the bench, chin in hands, elbows on knees, his teammates a blur of legs running by on the court in front of him.

Mrs. Tucker, the librarian, yelling at kids in front of her "Quiet Please" sign.

They are not flattering—but they are real. Almost beautiful in a strange way. Like some modern-day Norman Rockwell painting of dirty-kneed rule-breakers. Meaningful, candid moments of real life. Every image affects me in some way. Stirs me. Each one . . . emotionally charged. That's it. Ms. Carter always encourages us to write in an "emotionally charged" way, to capture a moment of something really good or really bad, but full of raw feeling. Isabelle's yearbook has pictures of those typical high school highs, but Xander and his camera—he has somehow captured the lows.

"Did you . . ." I pick up a stack and shuffle through them, "did you take all of these?"

A hairline X appears in the bottom right corner of every one. A criss-cross crack. His signature, or a broken lens, perhaps.

"Most are for my Yearbook assignment." He glances at Isabelle. "I thought if I took a lot, I'd have a better chance of getting what she wanted."

Isabelle holds up a photo of a grade 7 vomiting all over his lunchbox as the kids around him recoil at the splatter. "Seriously. Like, who wants to keep that memory?" Disgusted, she tosses it back in the pile. "Don't you get it? No one wants to see this—much less remember it."

"But it happened," he argues. "It's true."

She sighs. "Why can't you do more pictures like this one?" She holds up a shot of a girl sitting alone on a swing. She looks sad, to be honest, but it might pass for daydreaming. "Or the good stuff?"

"Why do people only want to remember the good things?" he asks. "That's only half the story. And Mrs. O'Neill said telling half a story is like lying. You need to tell the whole truth."

Xander picks up another photo and considers it. "Why don't people want to see pain or sadness? It's real." He flips the photo around to show us Hogan, sullen and smoking on the school steps. "Right, Hogan?"

HOGAN

t's me, all right. Smoking on the school steps, alone in a blur of kids coming and going. I'm the only thing in focus. Which is kinda cool. Cigarette in hand, smoke seeping through my lips, clouding my face—but you can still tell it's me. I look pretty badass.

Xander looks at it. "My grandfather told me, 'This guy is a rebel. He's pushing people away, but what he really wants is for someone to care.'"

I snatch it from Xander's hand to rip it up. But something catches my eye and I bring it closer for a better look.

The jean jacket.

"If you really wanted to be alone," Xander goes, "why are you sitting on the steps?"

"Yeah," Izzy adds. "Why'd you even come? It wasn't for school."

I remember now—the day I wore his jacket. October 16.

I clench my jaw. Take a deep breath. "It was Randy's anniversary."

No one says anything.

"My parents went to the cemetery . . ." I swallow, "but I couldn't."

I still haven't. Haven't even cried. Not once. What kind of stone-cold bastard doesn't cry over his own brother?

I keep my eyes on the picture. "So, I came to school. I sat on the steps all morning. Never went to a class. Never even spoke to anyone. But I had nowhere else to go."

I feel him then, Randy, the weight of him on my chest, his hands locked around my throat like when we were kids.

Give up, Hulkster? You can't win.

It happens whenever I think of him. I stop, take a couple more breaths, and it goes away. But he'll be back. He always is.

"I wore his jean jacket. I'd lost mine and it was cold that day." I remember taking it from the closet, the smell of him still on it. The ghost of him in it. Mom had finally given away all his stuff, but she'd forgotten about his jacket. And when I slipped it on, it was like he was there behind me, arms around me just ready to tackle me to the ground.

"What are you looking at in the photo?" Alice asks, leaning in. "What's in your hand?"

It's a small square between my fingers, but I know exactly what it is. "My football card. I was looking for my smokes and I found it in his pocket." I shake my head and toss the picture back on the pile. "Yeah—like he was pointing the finger from the grave."

"Or maybe," Alice says, so quiet I can barely hear her, "like Isabelle said, maybe he was just a proud brother."

"Is that . . .?" Izzy snatches a picture from the pile on the floor and glares at Xander. "You said you destroyed that picture."

"I did," Xander goes. "This one is a different shot."

"Wilson meant all of them." She frowns as she looks at it. "You should've destroyed them all."

145

"But he specifically said: 'Destroy this picture and its negative.'" Xander seems confused. "That is not that picture."

I sneak a look at the photo in her hand: a close-up of a girl sitting at a table, face hidden behind the curtain of hair, X-acto knife in her fingers. Sunlight catches on the tiny triangle blade waiting over her smooth inner arm.

It's beautiful. And terrible. All at the same time. Dramatic. Just like Izzy.

"We can't see your face," I say, trying to help. "It could be anyone."

She rips it in tiny pieces and throws them in the trash. "Yeah. But it IS me."

"It's you, then," Alice goes. "It's just one moment."

"Yes. YES!" Xander looks at her. His eyes light up. "One moment. You see that, you get it, right, Alice?"

Alice blushes.

"Easy for you to say, Alice," Izzy says. "It's not your moment that's exposed. It's like . . . I'm naked."

Normally, I would have made some smartass comment about seeing her naked, but not now. I know what she means. I felt like that when everyone was staring at my picture. Like they were seeing that hidden part that no one should. A part of me that even I had never seen before.

I look at the photos sprawled all over the floor. The hundreds of naked moments Xander saw but everyone else missed. He's weird, but somehow he seems different to me. Like, I'm seeing him more clearly, too.

"How do you do that?" I ask. "Time it just right, I mean, to catch that moment."

He looks at me like I've said something ridiculous. "I dunno."

"Is it something you learned in Photography class?" Alice asks.

Xander shrugs. "I just watch." He picks up his camera and looks through it. Lowers it and adjusts the lens. "They happen all the time. Most people are so caught up in their moment they don't see all the ones happening around them, I guess."

It makes sense. I've been so busy with my Randy stuff, I had no idea Izzy was so stressed, that she was cutting. Hell, I didn't even know she's adopted.

"You're creeping them." Izzy waves her hand at the pile of pictures. "Invading privacy."

Xander shakes his head. "I only see what's there for everyone to see. The Yearbook classroom door was open. Hogan was sitting on the school steps." Xander lists the facts like it's so obvious to him. "If you do something out in the open, why are you upset when people see it? Like Facebook. Or Instagram. You put up pictures of yourself on vacation in your red-and-white-striped bikini. So, why am I a creep for looking at them?"

Izzy crosses her arms over her chest. Rolls her eyes. Her typical answer when she hasn't got one.

He has a point, though. She always puts up selfies. Pictures of her pouting and posing in different outfits, or lying on her bed, or trying new hairstyles or makeup. As though her hotness depends on getting enough likes.

"Anyone could see these things," Xander points at his pictures, "if they zoomed in like the Tank does. It all depends on what you focus on."

XANDER

Writer's Craft Journal
Xander Watt
March 30, 2016

ASSIGNMENT: Extended Metaphor Poem.

The world makes sense
through my camera lens.

Because film doesn't lie
like people do.

The Tank
    Shows what is.
    Frames my vision.

Makes me focus.
Helps me see
reel life.

Truths exposed in black and white.
Where even shades of gray are clear.

And in my solitary darkness,
understanding slowly develops.

But I'll never know why
optimists claim to know
"the big picture."

Because it can not exist without
the negative.

ALICE

"It's not on Instagram or whatever . . . so no one else but us will ever see it," I say to Isabelle, trying to ease her embarrassment. "Right, Xander?"

He nods soberly, and then, as though having an epiphany, suddenly starts rummaging through his mess of pictures on the floor. "Wait! Wait! I have another one."

"See?" Isabelle whines.

"It's not a big deal," I say, trying to help her keep things in perspective. "It's just a photograph, so—"

"No, no," Xander interrupts, excitedly, like he can't wait to show me. "This one's of you, Alice."

Me?

Unease ripples through me at the thought of what he might produce—but wait, this is me. Invisible, boring me. What has he possibly captured that would be of any interest?

"Here." He pulls one from the pile and hands it to me.

Me. Alone at a long lunch table. Students, a blur around me. I remember that day. Noah was home sick and I had no reason, no excuse to eat in the High Needs room. I even stopped by to eat with Kim or help out with the other students, but they were all gone on a class trip so I went to the caf. The photo catches my uneaten tuna sandwich in my hand, my slumped shoulders, my stare into the emptiness across from me. It catches that moment, the day I realized what had long been true.

I am alone. Completely alone.

Isabelle glances at it. "See? Who wants to see that in a yearbook? Who wants to remember that? It's just sad."

And it is. I am. Pitiful, really. My throat tightens.

God, am I going to cry? Here? Now? Over a lunchroom picture? That's even more pathetic.

I get it now. Why Isabelle and Hogan reacted so strongly. The truth is there in black and white. Literally. But Xander isn't to blame. All he did was hold up the mirror and show us what we'd rather not see.

And it's not just that I am by myself for lunch that day—I am alone, more alone than I care to admit. Sure, I have Gran. And Noah. But when Gran dies, I'll be Noah's everything. And I will. I love my brother, I do. But it's just so . . . so one-sided. Noah just can't engage like typical people. He leans in, if he's calm, when I hug him, but he doesn't hug me. He doesn't ask how my day was. He doesn't care about me. Not really. Sometimes, I wonder if he even knows who I am.

When Gran is gone, I'll care for Noah like I promised. But who will care about me?

I look back at the photo. I was thinking about my mother that day as I watched other kids eating—or tossing out—the sandwiches their moms made. Wondering what it would've been like to have a mom that cared. How ironic that while most teens wish their mom would give them space, what I most want is for mine to give a crap.

She came home for Grampa's funeral the week before Xander took that photo. I hadn't seen her in ten years. Had hardly heard from her, aside from a few postcards now and then. She's a stranger to me. And though I stayed still while Noah rocked and bobbed, I was just as agitated by her presence as Grampa's absence.

After years of longing for her, I couldn't wait to see her again. To reconnect. But even as she hugged us, she didn't look at us with love or even interest. Her eyes held only shame. I overheard her arguing with Gran in the kitchen that night when I was coming back down the stairs to get my journal. I stood there, hand on the railing, needing to hear what, on some level, I already knew.

"They're your children, Shelly. Your kids." I heard Gran tapping her spoon on the edge of her teacup like she always did after she stirred things up.

"I can't, Mom." My mother's voice was low. "Things are . . . complicated right now."

Gran paused. "You've been saying that for nearly fifteen years. Life is complicated, girl. You just do the best you can with what you've got. Look at me."

"That's why they're with you. This is the best place for them." She paused. "Besides, with Dad gone . . . you'll be needing their help with the kennels."

Gran sighed. "I'm getting old, Shelly. I won't always be here." She paused. "And what then?"

What then?

I've been asking myself that all this past year. Gran is strong. Healthy. She might outlive us all. But what if she doesn't.

What then?

"Look, Mom," my mother finally said, "I've got my own life to live. One that doesn't have space for kids with . . . needs. Needs I just can't meet."

I realized a truth on the stairwell that night. I didn't stir love or pride in my mother. Not even a vague concern or detached curiosity, as I might from a kind stranger. That night I had an epiphany and it shook me to the core: the only thing I ever made my mom feel was guilt.

Even now, it wasn't about her kids. It was about her. We were simply her mistakes. Me and Noah. And the mistake wasn't leaving us, it was having us in the first place.

Standing in the shadows on the stairs, I promised myself that I would never abandon my family, Noah and Gran, for now they were all the family I had. My mother had given me life, given me a brother, and then given me away. She was weak and irresponsible, selfish, plain and simple.

And I swore that night that I would never be anything like her.

ISABELLE

"**S**ee?" I say, as he gives Alice her terrible photo.

She looks like she's going to cry. Obviously she took what I said the wrong way. I meant that the photo was sad—not her. But yeah, now that I look at it again, she is a total Eeyore. Pretty depressing. So is the way she's just sitting there now, staring at the photo like that droopy donkey, moaning, Oh well . . . guess I've got no one to sit with at lunch.

Some problem.

"At least you're not doing something secret in the photo," I say, trying to help out. I mean, come on. Reality check, people. "Even your picture, Hogan. It's just you guys sitting on the steps or in the caf where everyone can see you anyway. They're not as bad as my picture. Not by far."

"It's not a contest, Iz," Hogan says. "Why do you always have to make it about you?"

It's not the first time someone has said that to me. But Hogan says it differently. Like a real question that he wants me to answer. Only, for the first time ever, I don't have a comeback.

"What?" I say, confused. Because, honestly, it feels like it's never about me. Not the real me, anyway. "I don't always make it about me. Do I? I mean, seriously . . . is that what you guys think?"

The question hangs there between us, growing heavier with each passing second.

"Yeee-ah," Hogan says, drawing it out like it's SO obvious.

"Alice?" I ask. Surely, she doesn't think so. I mean, the girl has clearly idolized me since, like, grade school.

She looks up from her downer zone-out. Blushes a bit. "Ummm . . ." She looks apologetic, and already I feel myself cringing. "You maybe . . . sometimes act . . . a bit like you sort of . . ."

"Tell her the truth, Alice," Hogan says. "She asked for it."

Alice bites her lip and then continues in a gush of words. "You're just very . . . egocentric." She pauses and smiles slightly. "No offense."

"What do you mean by that?" I ask, genuinely confused but thinking I really should be offended.

Alice hesitates and looks at the others.

"Egocentric," Dictionary Dork chimes in, "self-centered, self-absorbed. Acting like the world revolves around you."

Then Hogan adds his two cents. "You act like you matter more than everyone else at St. F.X."

"I'm School Pres-i-dent," I say, spelling it out for them. Don't they get it? I do matter more, in a way, because I have way more responsibility than any other student. All they have to worry about is their classes. I've got all of that and dances and sports, and running Student Council practically on my own. Anything goes wrong, it's on me. Any event, I have to plan, emcee, and somehow photograph for the yearbook that I'm, oh yeah, also putting together. "All the extra stuff that happens at St. F.X.— the spirit weeks, planning your freaking prom—do you think all that just . . . just happens? Do you have any idea how many hours I put into—?"

"You're doing it again," Hogan says.

I take a deep breath. "I'm not talking about me. I'm talking about all the stuff, all the work I do . . . for you."

"For me?" he asks.

"For all of you."

Hogan looks around at the other pair. "Hands up," he smirks, "who's been to a dance?"

Alice and Xander shake their heads.

"Spirit Week—you guys into that?"

They keep shaking.

"What about you, Noah?" he asks over his shoulder to the guy spazzing out in the corner. "Prom? . . . Anybody?"

Embarrassed, Alice and Xander look away.

I glare at Hogan. "That doesn't prove anything except that you're all a bunch of antisocial loners with, like, zero school spirit." This time I don't say "no offense." Screw them. Let them get offended for a change. My head throbs. I feel another meltdown coming on. The seal has been broken. Already the tears are burning behind my eyes.

"We didn't mean to upset you, Isabelle," Alice says.

"It's just high school," Hogan adds. "In the big picture, none of this really matters."

And just like that, he voices what I've been fearing all along, what I realized on my trip: all my striving, all my efforts to impress, to succeed, to be perfect—it doesn't matter. None of it does.

I wasn't happy before DREX, but I was in denial. I believed I'd be satisfied with the next win, the next party, the perfect relationship, the perfect prom. But if I'm honest, none of those things are enough.

And if that's not my purpose—then what is?

"At least I'm trying; I'm doing something," I say, my lip trembling. "What have any of you ever done for your school?"

No one speaks. Xander goes back to his stack of photos. Hogan picks at his nails. Alice tosses her picture back into the pile.

"Whatever." I cross my arms and lean against the wall. "I was just trying to help—with school activities, with yearbook, with Alice and her stupid picture. It's like I said—no matter what I do, it's not enough. I give up."

"No," Alice says, "I get it. I do. You are the heart of the school. What would St. F.X. be without Isabelle Parks?"

I think she means it. The heart of the school. My eyes soften a bit. What would this school be without me? But the real question is: who will I be without St. F.X.?

"Oh, here's Noah's." Xander interrupts us with another picture.

It's Noah in the hallway, being wrestled to the ground by two staff members as Wilson yells into his walkie-talkie. Whatever setting Xander used blurs the chaos but somehow focuses on Noah's face—on the terror, the confusion, but especially the rage. He looks wild. Insane. Dangerous.

"What the hell is going on there?" Hogan leans in for a closer look.

"He has meltdowns, sometimes," Alice says, like that explains it. "If he gets . . . overwhelmed."

In the corner, Noah starts tapping his head, muttering to himself, growing more and more restless. He slaps himself hard a few times as he makes this weird squawk. The room feels very small, and I glance at the door, our only exit, wedged shut.

"He's fine, he'll be fine," Alice says. But I'm not sure if she is reassuring me or herself.

NOAH

Waves
over the horizon.
I hear them come, watch
them grow from ripple to roar.
I kick.
Spit. Scratch.
Scream.
I fight cresting
white, frothy madness,
but I cannot stop the
crash.
I lose myself
inside the wave.
It swallows me whole.
Drowns me in sights and sounds—
Suffocating.

Out!
I need out.
I need to run.
AWAY!
NOW!
But something, someone,
always holds me here.
Holds me down.
No matter how hard
I cry for
help.

ALICE

've seen a thousand meltdowns, each of them distressing in one way or another, but seeing it in one frame, one moment, somehow makes it even harder.

Hogan takes the photo and examines it. "That's pretty extreme. Does it happen a lot?"

"No," I say. "That day was the worst one. They called a Secure School because of it."

"That's why we had it?" Isabelle looks back, fearful. "Is he . . . dangerous?"

I don't know how to answer that. "He isn't dangerous, well, not really." It doesn't sound convincing. "He's more dangerous to himself, if anything. He could get hurt thrashing around like that. Or hurt someone."

Isabelle's eyes widen.

"By accident," I add quickly.

"Have you ever been hurt?" she asks.

"Not on purpose," I say, vaguely.

The truth is, I've been on the receiving end of Noah's outbursts a few times. Many times. All my life, really. When he gets frustrated he scratches. Slaps. Bites. Pulls my hair if he can get at it. One time, he even broke my arm when he flipped the table.

"He doesn't mean it," I explain. "I should have known better. Should have given him his space."

Over the years, I learned how to steer clear, just like our dogs do. They sense Noah's episodes, feel it coming like a thunderstorm and make themselves scarce, hiding out in the basement or under the furniture. Now that Noah is so much bigger than me and Gran, we have locks on our bedroom doors. When Grampa screwed in the bolts last fall, he said the locks were to keep special things safe—I see now, now that he's gone, he wasn't talking about my china doll collection. He meant me and Gran.

"How do you handle his . . . meltdowns?" Isabelle asks. "I mean, you're pretty scrawny. No offense."

She's right. I am small. Slender. Slight. Okay, scrawny.

"I usually try to corral him into his safe zone. He'll wind down on his foam floor or exercise ball or wrap up in his blankets," I say, realizing that none of those are options now. "But if it's really bad, I lock myself in my room and wait him out."

"Like a lockdown?" Hogan says, and snorts.

But it isn't funny.

"Yeah . . ." I choke on the truth of it. "I guess my whole life is a lockdown."

We sit in silence listening to the click of the switch as Noah flicks the lights on and off.

Click.

Click.

Click.

Click.

I feel stupid for speaking it—even if it is my reality. My life is a lockdown. What kind of pathetic soul admits that out loud?

"I know what you mean," Hogan says, interrupting my inner critic.

"Totally," Isabelle adds.

It surprises me. Do they, really? Only someone living my story would truly know.

"I shut everyone out after Randy died," Hogan says, looking at his picture.

Nobody speaks.

"It's like . . ." Isabelle struggles to find the right words. "Like we lock up a part of ourselves out of fear. Fear of being judged. Fear of failing."

". . . or fear of getting hurt," I say.

". . . or of hurting someone else," Hogan adds.

". . . or of always being alone," Xander says in his robotic way, as he continues to sort through the pile of photos.

Our personalities, our stories are so very different—and yet, our fears feel so similar.

I look around the tiny washroom. The five of us cooped up and locked down. And Noah, humming, moaning, flicking the lights on and off.

Click-click-click.

Trapped, as his unspoken fears wind tighter.

Tighter.

Tighter.

How long do we have, I wonder, before he finally snaps?

HOGAN

"**H**ere it is." Xander hands me a photo.

I'm afraid it's gonna be another Hallmark moment in my loser life. But it isn't me. It's the guy from the yearbook, Maxwell what's-his-name. Same skinny guy, same geeky shirt, same just-try-me expression. Like he wants you to hit him. Same everything, really, except for the guns.

Yes, guns. Two of them, actually.

He's standing on a bluff, one large rifle slung over his back, the other butted up against his shoulder. It's not the ammo belt criss-crossing the rifle strap, or even the guns that get me. They're only paintball guns, painted black to look more realistic. Randy and I often went paintballing when we were young and, as usual, I'd come out covered in yellow, splattered and stained by his many bull's-eyes. Those paint pellets sting and bruise, but they aren't dangerous. Not really. Well, not if you're wearing the gear.

I look back at this guy's face, uneasy. No, it isn't about the guns. It's him. Maxwell. The way he holds his rifle, one eye sighting down the black barrel, taking aim at the camera.

At me.

Something twists in my gut as I think how this guy is loose and trigger-happy in our halls where hundreds of students and teachers hide in dark rooms. They don't know what's going on. Even the cops don't. Not really. They might have his name, but they don't have this picture. They don't know who they're dealing with. But I do. I've seen that expression before. Randy had it right before he jumped on me. A face that says: you're gonna get it, bad.

My stomach clenches again. Fear. That's what that is. A sensation I haven't felt in such a long time. Not since Randy. I thought I'd already faced the worst. Lived it. Nothing scares you, no threat or consequence works when you have already lost everything. But this guy's cocky smirk, his dark eyes, winking as he takes aim—it says he's serious. Something about his expression scares the crap out of me. Not for my sake, but for everyone in this building. For Izzy. For Alice and Noah. And even Xander. I feel afraid, but most of all, I feel helpless.

And that is even worse.

"Ohmigod!" Izzy snatches the photo from my hand and examines it closely. "Are those GUNS?!"

Noah stops bobbing and paces around the small circuit. Hums louder. He's obviously getting agitated by Izzy's screeching. We all are.

"Paintball guns," I say.

Her eyes go wide. "Well, they sure look real."

"The cops know who he is." I try to sound calmer than I feel. Like it's no biggie. "They'll get him. Don't worry."

Alice takes the picture from Izzy and looks closely. Her face pales. She sees his look; she feels it too.

"He saw you, didn't he?" She looks up at Xander. "Maxwell saw you take this picture."

Xander nods, but doesn't say anything more.

"Are you, like, totally crazy?" Izzy blurts. "It's one thing to creep us." She looks back at the photo and shivers. "But this guy had guns. GUNS! He saw you, Xander. And you just take his picture? Geez, he could have killed you!"

Noah stops circling and begins slapping his head, rocking on his feet like he's gonna start a race but changes his mind.

Go.

Stop.

Go.

Stop.

Like a never-ending loop of false starts.

ISABELLE

Noah is totally spazzing out in the corner, waving his arms, flapping his hands, moaning like he's in pain. And he's getting worse. I glance at the stall. I could lock myself in there. I mean, the guy's own grandfather made panic rooms for them. Obviously, he's not safe to be around.

Alice jumps up and I think she's going for the stall. But instead she goes over to Noah.

"You're okay. Noah. You're okay," she says, her voice trying to stay calm. Her hands are up like she's gentling a wild horse. "We're going to go to the bus soon. Five minutes. Okay?"

He tilts his head like he's just heard a strange sound far away and he stops waving to pull at his hair. But the rocking doesn't stop and his groaning is getting louder.

Why doesn't she do something? "Can't you shut him up?"

"You're the one that set him off," Hogan says to me.

Alice picks up his broom and offers it to him. "Want to sweep, Noah?"

But as she steps forward, instead of taking it from her, his arms explode outward and he screams.

"YeeEEEEEEEaaargh!"

Total freak-out. Like a tornado of fists and spit as his arms windmill around him like crazy propellers. Alice tries to step back, but there isn't anywhere else to go. The broom wedges under the sink and Noah's next swing catches her smack in the face, sending her staggering back, and she falls to the ground.

SNAP!

Ohmigod! Her arm? Her neck?

I rush over to her. "Are you okay?"

Noah is revving up by the second, yelling, fists flailing as he moves towards us. But before I can scream, Hogan comes barreling into him.

HOGAN

"**D**on't think," Coach always says, "just act. Trust your gut." And my gut told me: Shut this guy down. Whatever it takes.

But as soon as I tackle Noah, drive him to the floor, and squeeze him tight, ready for his worst—he stops. The screaming, the thrashing—it all stops, and he relaxes into me like we're just two dudes hugging on the bathroom floor.

"You okay?" I ask Alice over my shoulder from where we lie.

Izzy helps her stand. Alice seems fine, a bit shaken up, but okay. The broom handle is in two pieces on the floor.

"Yeah," she says, looking at her face in the mirror. "I think so."

"Ohmigod!" Izzy goes. "I thought you broke your neck or something!"

I nod at the red welt on Alice's cheek. "You're gonna have a nice shiner there."

"Yeah." She tests it with her fingertips and looks in the

mirror. "Wouldn't be the first time. No concussion, though. I should've known better. I was too close." She turns and looks at Noah. But there's no accusation, no anger, not even fear. Just softness. "It was an accident." She looks at me, her welt angry but her eyes gentle. "Accidents happen. He didn't mean it. That's what counts."

I don't know if she's saying it for Noah, or if he even understands, but I do. I get it. For the first time—I hear it.

Noah starts nuzzling the fur on my arm. If he knows he hurt Alice, he's already forgotten. I wish I could think like him. I wish it were that easy for me.

"I think he likes you, Hogan," Izzy teases, like it's a crazy thing. I guess it is, really.

Noah rubs his face against my fur, turning his head in circles and sideways like a cat. I half expect him to start purring. It is the weirdest thing: the Hulk—school badass and loner—in a furry costume, lying on the bathroom floor, bear-hugging this retar—autistic kid. But I don't mind it. Not at all.

And that is even weirder.

Click.

"Okay, Noah." Alice rests her hand on his. "We're going to sit now."

I loosen my grip a bit, but I'm ready for him if he starts freaking again. He doesn't. In fact, he's like a different kid, not the twister we had in here a few seconds ago. Alice bends down and picks up the top half of the broom handle. It's about eight inches long, but the "Noah" tag is still on it, and when he takes it and sits beside her, he seems happy enough to hold it and flick the tag back and forth and back and forth.

Izzy smiles. "Looks like you've been replaced, Hogan."

I run my hand over the back of my head as I sit up. "Wouldn't be the first time."

It's out before I know it, and her smile slips off her face. She looks away.

That wasn't fair. I shouldn't have said that. I mean, it was just one kiss. Not like we were dating or serious. But I thought she liked me.

What an idiot.

Like me? She hardly even knew me, really, and after Randy's accident, I stopped trying. What was I thinking, anyway? Me and Isabelle Parks? We didn't have to break up, because we were never together, not really. I just stopped returning her calls. Deleted her "u doing ok?" texts. Ignored her looks of pity. That wasn't how I wanted her to look at me anyway, and soon enough, Izzy stopped looking at me at all.

XANDER

Writer's Craft Journal

Xander Watt

April 4, 2016

ASSIGNMENT: Describe an inciting incident in your life—a pivotal moment when everything changed.

My Inciting Incident

I work at Comic Corner part-time. Actually, it started out as a co-op placement last semester. It was Mrs. O'Neill's idea. She knows I love comics. Especially Star Wars comics. I only ever read Star Wars until I met Maxwell Steinberg. He worked there after school and he would be coming in for his shift as I was leaving.

In the beginning, I didn't say much to him or anyone, really. There weren't a lot of customers in the small store. The few that came in only asked me questions I could answer easily, like

- Where can I find *Deadpool* #65?
- Did my *Mighty Avengers* come in?
- Where is the bathroom?

The owner, John Banks, spent a lot of time on his computer and only asked me questions like

- Did you put the posters up?
- Can you move the back issues into the bins?
- Do you want to take your break now?

So, I was free to do what I like best: organize comics. I am very good at organizing things and I know how to handle a comic book correctly. Mrs. O'Neill also thought it would be a good job for me because it would help me with small talk.

small talk
/ˈsmɔl ˌtɔk/
noun: polite conversation about unimportant things

I don't get small talk. It's basically people asking other people silly questions. It's talking about things you don't really care about with people you don't really care about. It doesn't make sense. Why would I care if some stranger at the bus stop thinks it's a nice day?

But it didn't matter much, because there was not a lot of small talk at Comic Corner. And I liked that just fine.

I noticed a few things the first time I saw Maxwell Steinberg standing at the counter sorting the new stock. First, he was about the same size as me. Second, he had a neat T-shirt with nine heroes on it, all Marvel, not DC. And last, the blue strip on his name tag had only three letters: MAX.

Maybe there was not enough space on the punch tape to spell the full name. But, no. Mine had ALEXANDER and that was nine letters long.

I pointed at his tag. "Isn't your name Maxwell?"

He looked at me funny. "Only my dad calls me that. And my teachers. And they're all assholes."

I considered his logic. If anyone using his real name was therefore an asshole, did that mean they were assholes because they used his name, or that typically all assholes use that name? And why do we call assholes "assholes," anyway? Because, anatomically speaking, an anus serves a very important purpose.

"Why are you staring at me?" he asked. I hadn't realized I was staring.

"Everyone needs an asshole," I finally said, "biologically speaking."

He shrugged. But he didn't walk away like most people did when I tried small talk.

"So, do you like the name Al-ex-an-der?" The way he said it, I decided that I did not.

"My preference is irrelevant," I said. "It's my name."

He laughed. If there was a joke, once again I'd missed it. Then he grabbed a stack of new comics and headed to the X-Men section. I followed. He moved down the New Releases shelf quickly placing his comics, one after another, in exactly the right places. I realized that he'd organized them first at the desk. By series. Then alphabetically. Then by issue.

I liked that.

"Anyone can change their name," he pointed at a few of the characters on the covers. "Cyclops, Iceman, Beast, Wolverine. All these characters did."

I hadn't realized that before. But, come to think of it, he was right.

"How about Al?" he said. "Or Alex?"

I shook my head. "That's my grandfather's name."

When he was finished with his comics, he peeled the blue strip from my name tag and ripped off a third of it. I was going to walk away, like Mrs. O'Neill said I should when I feel anxious. He'd just wrecked my name tag, and John Banks would not like it if I asked him to make another one. I had already asked because the letters were not spaced evenly and John Banks had said no.

But Max only threw part of the strip in the garbage. The other two thirds he stuck back on my name tag.

XANDER.

"There," he said. "How about that . . . Xander?"

I let the word bounce around in my head. Xander. Xan-DER. XAN-der.

I liked it. And I don't usually like change. But this was different. This was more like editing. Like what my English teacher said we should do. It was concise. Better. I smiled at Max.

Then he took a red Sharpie out of his back pocket. He traced over the X in my name and drew a circle around it. He didn't say anything else. But I knew. We were X-Men, me and Max—maX and Xander.

And I wondered if that meant we might be friends, too.

ALICE

A head injury. A gash on my leg. A black eye. Today is not my day. Not Noah's, either. He retreats into his mute aftermath, typical of his meltdowns, but the calm won't last long. The trigger is still there. He is still stuck in this room. It's only a matter of time before there's another outburst. A worse one.

He rolls his hat down over his eyes and taps his head against the stall. Yes, he has to get out of here.

Soon.

"I don't think Noah can last much longer in here," I admit.

"Me neither," Isabelle complains.

I look at the door, considering other options. "I could run with him. Maybe down the back stairs and out the side door."

"I dunno," Hogan says.

"Do you think it's just a prank?" Isabelle asks. "I mean, this guy Maxwell, do you think he's just trying to scare us? Or is he, like . . . totally crazy?"

Hogan stands and walks to the far corner just under the tiny window. He jumps up the wall and, after a few tries, manages to grab the ledge of the window well. Slowly he drags himself up to peek outside.

"What do you see?" I ask, as he hangs by one hand to open the latch. The glass is too dirty to see through but as the window tilts forward, he peers through the opening underneath.

Hogan pauses for a second, then drops to the ground. "Nothing, really. Just a few cop cars." He brushes his hands off on his fur. "But I think we oughta sit tight until Wilson says it's clear."

I know he saw something but I don't press him. Whatever it was is bad enough that he doesn't want to mention it.

I don't blame him. I've read enough about school shootings to know that if this isn't a prank, this Maxwell probably has a plan. Maybe even a list. Xander might be on it. Isabelle, for sure.

But I don't tell them that.

ISABELLE

BRI: Update. There's a second shooter!

IZZY: WTF? TWO?!

BRI: They said they could see another person with a gun on the atrium video, but it's not clear who.
He bolted before it showed his face.

IZZY: Do they know where he went?

BRI: They think he's hiding.
No sign of him since the atrium but I heard Maxwell is still setting off firecrackers, keeping the police away.

IZZY: Ya. We heard some. I thought it was gunshots.

BRI: Might be. They said he has a gun.

IZZY: So that second guy, he could be anywhere.
He could be anyone.

XANDER

November 5, 2015

Social Autopsy #69

Event: X-Men Secrets

Today Max asked me to help him with a secret. At first, I thought it was for John Banks' birthday. Maybe even a Dairy Queen cake—but I was hoping not the kind with chunky bits. I don't like things in my ice cream.

Turns out the secret wasn't cake—but it was something much better. Max told me to meet him by the school dumpster at 9:30 p.m. and to bring my camera. Most importantly, he made me promise not to tell anyone, beause it wasn't just a secret. It was a secret mission.

I've read all the *X-Men* comics. They're my new favorites. But

I still wasn't sure what to wear for a secret mission. A cape? A utility belt? A black unitard? Max never said. The only thing I could find was Grandpa Alex's old wraparound sunglasses.

Mom was at work. It was easy to sneak out. I wasn't sure why Max wanted to meet at the school. Everything was closed. And why did he need my camera? I wore my black T-shirt and jeans. My Cyclops glasses. It was so dark with them on, I had to pop out the lenses just to see. I took one of my X-Men stickers and stuck it on the arm of the glasses. A big red X in a circle.

Max laughed when I met him at the dumpster.

"Nice glasses—they belong to Grandpa Alex?"

How did he know?

I wondered if Max had empathic powers, too. I noticed he was not wearing glasses or a utility belt. Just a backpack. But maybe he was more like Wolverine. Maybe his mutant powers only came out when he most needed them.

Mr. Dean, the janitor, exited through the back door and headed for his Honda Civic. He must have been on evenings that week because I had not seen him cleaning up after lunch with Noah Waters the past few days. After he drove away, Max ran for the door. I thought it was locked, but Max had rigged up a little magnet that swung down when the door opened and wedged in to keep it from locking shut.

"You made that?" I asked. He smiled.

Yes, Max was very smart. I wanted to see how it worked, but he pulled me through the doors into the dark hallway.

I knew we were not supposed to be in there. But I couldn't leave now. Being with Max there in the darkness was like living a panel in a comic, not just reading them. I had to keep going to find out what came next.

I followed him down the dark corridors and up the three flights of stairs to Mr. Quigley's lab. I had Biology with Mr. Quigley during period 1. Mr. Quigley wore glasses and smelled like cigarettes. He was old and not very interested in teaching us anything other than what was on his next test. At the start o. the year, I'd asked a lot questions. I like to know things. How things work. Why. Where he got his facts. I also wanted to tell him what I knew about the subjects. Mr. Quigley did not like my questions or my help. I think he also needs stronger glasses because after a week or two, when he moved me to the back of the class, I don't think he could see me raising my hand. Luckily, I have an excellent memory. I remembered everything he told us and everything I read in the textbook. Otherwise, I would be failing.

"Did you forget your homework?" I asked Max. Maybe he was in Mr. Quigley's grade 11 Biology, period 2.

He didn't answer. Instead, he pulled out a set of keys. I'd have recognized that $E=MC^2$ lanyard anywhere; those were Mr. Quigley's keys. But where did Max get them? He unlocked the door and entered. Not wanting to stay in the dark hallway alone, I followed him inside.

We should not have been in the school after hours. We should not have been using Mr. Quigley's keys. I knew that. But I didn't know what Max had planned for our mission—and I just had to see.

Turning on the light, Max grabbed Mr. Quigley's lab coat from the hook. Then he dressed the skeleton with it. Then he unhooked the skeleton and laid it on its back on the long desk.

"Gimme your glasses," he said. So I did.

Max put them on the skull and then bent one of the skeleton's legs, so it looked like it was just suntanning on the desk. Then he took a cigarette from his pocket and wedged it between the teeth. Then he closed two fingers of the skeleton's hand, taped them together like an okay sign.

This did not look like any of the experiments we did in grade 11 Biology.

"Give me that big glass tube thing." Max nodded at the foot-long glass tube at the end of the counter.

"It's a graduated cylinder," I said, trying to be helpful. "It holds one thousand milliliters, but they come in different—"

"Whatever, Einstein. Just get it." He did not have a happy face. So I handed it to him.

He took a large bottle of Diet Pepsi from his backpack and opened it up.

"Can I have a sip?" I was pretty thirsty from running up the stairs.

But Max didn't answer. Instead, he filled the cylinder three-quarters full. Then he corked it with a rubber stopper he had rigged with paper clips, string, and four white Mentos candies.

I wondered what he was doing, but then he stepped back and I saw the skeleton wasn't just wearing Mr. Quigley's lab coat and sunglasses; it wasn't just smoking a cigarette as it leaned back against the books. It was jerking off its one thousand milliliter graduated cylinder.

Max laughed and he ran around the desk. He stood beside the skeleton, arm around it, and faced me. "Okay." He gave me the finger. "Take the picture."

"What?"

"Take my picture. Why do you think I brought you here, loser?" I wasn't sure, really. "Umm . . . for the sunglasses?"

"Take the damn picture!"

So I did. Even though it was kind of weird.

What kind of mission was this?

Max looked at the clock: 9:42. "The alarm defaults if the door hasn't locked fifteen minutes after it's set." Max jangled the keys. "I just gotta get a few more supplies." He disappeared through the back door marked "Private." And once again, I followed.

"We aren't really supposed to be in here," I said, as he scoured the shelves in the narrow room. Hundreds of glass bottles and jars stood in meticulously labeled rows. "Unless you're a Lab Tech. Are you a Lab Tech?"

He snorted as he unlocked the metal cabinet and took out a few jars, delicately placing them into his bag. "With those science suck-ups? Wasting their lunch hours cleaning out test tubes?" He opened another cabinet and took a few brown bottles. "No. Quigley didn't pick me. But I don't care. Who wants to be a stupid Lab Rat anyways?"

He closed the cabinets and locked up the supply room before hanging the keys around the skeleton's neck.

"Come on," he said. "We gotta hoof it. The alarm is gonna trigger soon."

"Shouldn't we . . .?" I looked at the obscene display on Mr. Quigley's desk. "I mean, don't we have to put away the, uh . . . lab equipment?"

It was Mr. Quigley's number-one rule. It felt terrible to me that we'd left the stuff out, all over his tests and marking, never mind what inappropriate things that skeleton was doing.

Max laughed again. "Stay if you want, but if you don't make it out the side door in three minutes, you'll be explaining all this to the cops."

He took off, shoes squeaking in the dimly lit hall as he bolted for the stairwell.

And I followed him. Like I'd followed him all evening.

But that's the thing with Max. I never know when he's joking or serious. I didn't understand the mission at all. And by the time he gave me a choice—there wasn't one, really.

Observations

1. The next morning, I was very nervous when I went to the lab, but surprisingly everyone liked Max's skeleton. In fact, they LOVED it. Even though it was wrong, the whole class thought it was so cool. They took photos and texted and tweeted.

    "Who did it?"

"Who's X?" they asked each other, looking at the Cyclops glasses.

I smiled. Proud. Bringing the glasses was my idea.

2. When Mr. Quigley arrived to class after his hall duty and saw the skeleton sprawled on his desk, he did not laugh or text or tweet. Mr. Quigley was mad. Like, off the charts, brain-vein-bulging mad. And when he grabbed the skeleton and tipped its graduated cylinder ever so slightly, the string released, and the Mentos hit the Diet Pepsi—and foam exploded, fizzing up and out of the glass tube and all over Mr. Quigley's purple face. Just the way Max had planned. And the kids all took pictures of it, just as Max had expected. And Max got his revenge, just as he'd hoped.

Conclusion

I know that breaking and entering was wrong. Leaving out the science equipment was wrong. And I'm sure whoever donated their skeleton to science did not mean for it to be used for this kind of social experiment. But in the big picture, which Mrs. O'Neill keeps telling me to look at—it was kind of funny.

I also know that stealing and lying is wrong. That's even in the Bible.

But since no one has asked me—I am not lying.

And since Max is my friend—I will keep his secret.

And if he asks to go on another secret mission, I might even say yes. And then, I won't need a Social Autopsy—in fact, I'll need to start a Mission Log.

00:16:04

HOGAN

Out of the corner of my eye, I see Iz shift closer to Alice. Something's up. She nudges her and tips her phone so Alice can read it. Obviously, they don't want me knowing, so I pretend like I didn't see.

There's stuff I don't want them knowing—like the dozen cop cars I saw in the parking lot. The yellow police tape holding back reporters. Or the ambulance waiting to deal with whatever might come next.

This is no prank.

"Hogan," Iz goes. "When you said that some kids wanted to leave school with a bang . . . what exactly did you mean by that?" For an actress, she's pretty horrible at acting casual. I guess for someone as dramatic as her, it's a big leap.

"I dunno. Nothing." I look at her directly. "Why?"

"Oh, just wondering." Izzy eyes the splintered wooden door

I kicked in, the stall door I pounded into place. "Where did you say you were when the shooting happened?"

"I didn't."

She looks at Alice. I know where this is going. And it's bullshit.

"It's just that . . . hypothetically," Alice says, "if there's more than one shooter, which, statistically, there usually is, the police will want to question anyone that wasn't in a classroom at the time of the shooting."

I glare at them. "Were any of you in class?"

They look away.

"I get it," I snap. "Of all the crazies in here," I wave my arm at Noah and Xander, "*hypothetically*, you guys assume it's me. Nice. Real nice." I snort and shake my head in disgust.

"Like I said," Izzy adds, "you are the one with a record. And you do have that . . ." she pulls in Alice once more, "how did you put it, Alice?"

Alice pauses.

"Alice?" Izzy elbows her.

Alice swallows and mumbles, "A hostile vibe."

"Hostile?" I blurt. Oh, this is rich. "So, why not Noah?" I point at the guy in the hat who's banging his head on the stall. "Of all the people in this room, *statistically*," I throw the word back at her, "he's the only one that has freaked out and injured someone today. Who's to say he didn't blow out the atrium and then go and hide in a closet? Because, *statistically*, he is the only one among us with a history of causing lockdowns!"

Izzy gasps. "He's right!" She eyeballs Noah.

But Alice isn't convinced. In fact, she's pissed. "You've got to be joking!" She gets up and stands right in front of me. "You can't seriously be blaming Noah . . . for this?"

Click.

XANDER

wondered what Max had taken from the lab supply cabinet. But I didn't have to wonder long. The next week, he told me to meet him outside the caf at lunch. No one had ever asked to meet me for lunch. I was pretty excited. I even brought an extra Twinkie for him.

I didn't think he was going to show, but he did. Only he didn't have his lunch. Just a remote, like the one from my new plane. It was based on the Lockheed SR-71 spy plane, just like the X-Men jet. I'd just gotten it for my birthday, and when Max heard, he'd asked if he could borrow it. I did not want to lend it. But #4 on Mrs. O'Neill's Friendship Checklist says that friends share. So I did.

191

I followed him in the side door, up the shadowy stairs, and onto the dark stage. Through the thick navy curtain I could hear the sounds of the kids having lunch in the cafetorium on other side.

My stomach growled. "So, are we going to eat? I brought you a—"

"Take my picture first." Max picked up a plane, MY plane, resting at his feet.

I was happy to see he'd brought my X-Jet back in one piece. Even if he'd painted our red X symbol on it. That was cool.

I guess.

I took his picture, unsure of why he even wanted me to. He never asked to see them. I tried to show him once and he told me to keep them top secret.

The cafetorium was full of kids, and teachers on duty watching the kids eat. And Principal Wilson watching the teachers watch the kids eat. And while everyone was busy watching each other, Max knelt down just behind the curtain crack and shoved the plane out center stage. Working the remote, he made it do a vertical takeoff, though I could have done one way better, and then he sent the X-Jet out over the crowd.

He should have asked me to fly it. He was not a very good pilot. Plus he'd rigged up little test tubes along the bottom that were weighing it down. Clearly he had not read the instruction manual I'd given him. I hoped he had not ignored my directions about not tearing up the box, too.

This friendship thing was a lot harder than I'd expected.

By the time a kid noticed the plane, it was halfway across the cafetorium. Everyone looked up laughing as it swooped overhead, and they all started chanting, "X-Jet! X-Jet! X-Jet!"

Principal Wilson shouted for it to land NOW and the room went silent. All except for the drone of the X-Jet now on a collision course with him. It dive-bombed, making him duck as it pulled up at the last second. Kids cheered as the jet rose higher and higher.

"Fire in the hole!" Max said beside me as the near-vertical plane tipped enough to unload the contents of the tubes.

It wasn't much liquid, really. But as it hit the principal he gasped and retched. Kids around him bolted, pinching their noses, gagging at the smell. I knew even before the stench reached us it was BTA—butyric acid taken from the science lab. It wasn't dangerous. Like Mr. Quigley said, it's found in the colon and in body odor and milk and parmesan cheese. But BTA is best known for being in, and smelling like, vomit. Strong vomit. Like burn-your-nose-hairs vomit.

Mr. Wilson ran for the doors, retching like Misty, my neighbor's cat. But he'd never get away from the smell. Not for days.

"Mission accomplished," Max said, dropping the remote as he got up to leave. I looked through the curtains, just as my X-Jet smashed into the basketball backboard and dropped. Half of it dangled in the white netting, the rest of it fell in shattered pieces to the floor. Max cheered, as though he'd done it on purpose. As though even that was part of his plan.

It wasn't, was it?

Did he even have a plan—or was he just figuring it out as he went? But before I could ask, he'd gone.

I won't lie. I was mad. Almost crying when I saw that plane crash. But as I write this mission log tonight, I'm trying to do what Max says I need to do. Max says I'm too focused on silly things. And maybe he's right. Sure, the Tank helps me zoom in and focus—but maybe I should think more like Max. He sees the big picture, even if I can't. He's got a plan. And if I want to be a part of it, I just have to trust him.

Besides, Cyclops crashed the real X-Jet a bunch of times. And I've never seen him cry.

XANDER

Max and I waited in my hiding spot—the corner carrel. I told him it was my secret place where I read my Star Wars graphic novels sometimes. And just like I said she would, Mrs. Tucker turned out the lights and left for lunch at 11:07.

We climbed off the desk and Max pulled three tinfoil things out of his backpack. They each had a foot-long silver shaft and three round bulbs at the bottom. He held one up against his crotch and told me to check out his foil dick. Technically, a penis should have only two testicles. I wondered if he knew that. I wondered if, perhaps, he had three.

He told me to take his picture. So I did, even though it was weird. But lots of kids do things other people think is weird—like how Danny obsesses over medieval weapons, or Trisha collects fishing lures, or how I know everything there is to know about Star Wars. Like Mrs. O'Neill says, everyone has unique interests. Maybe genitalia was Max's thing. He'd done that skeleton thing, and now this. Come to think of it, a lot of kids seemed to enjoy drawing them in our textbooks and on the bathroom stalls. I wondered how long he'd been interested in the art of penises. So I asked him. He just looked at me funny.

"Or is it penii?" I corrected myself.

Max said I was messed up (even though he was the one with three testicles) and asked me for the stickers. My job had been to make a sheet of X-Men stickers. Big, red, circled Xs. Max said every superhero leaves a calling card. All this time, I'd thought it was just the villains. But he didn't even thank me. He stuck them on the three foil shafts and told me to keep a lookout while he climbed up to put them on the bookshelves. Then he hung strips like flypaper from a few ceiling sprinklers. I looked down the hall for Mrs. Tucker, who I knew would not like Max's decorating.

After a few seconds, the air reeked of burning plastic or hair. Then Max grabbed my arm and ran for the emergency exit at the back. I tried to tell him it was alarmed, but the thick black smoke chugging from the silver shafts caught my eye.

"Max, your penii are on fire!" I yelled. But he didn't seem to care. The strips above them burned like fuses towards the sprinklers. But before I could tell him, the fire alarm sounded, the sprinklers turned on, and Max shoved open the alarmed door and dragged me out behind him. My heart raced as we joined all the kids and teachers filing out of the school. Everyone was freaking out.

"I see smoke."

"Something's burning."

"Is there a fire?"

Only Max and I knew the truth. It made me feel smart to know something the other kids didn't. But I felt kind of sick, too. Those were some serious rules we'd just broken. We stood with the crowds gathered on the football field, shuffling and stomping in the snow. Max shushed me when I told him we could have stayed inside where it was warm, because we knew there wasn't really a fire, and the school was totally empty so no one would have seen us, and the firemen always took seven minutes.

Then Max smiled and said I was brilliant. I wasn't sure what I'd said, exactly. All that mattered was how happy it made Max.

Six and a half minutes later, the fire truck came, and firemen ran into the building, axes ready. All because of Max's three tin-foil penii. I wish he'd told me his plan, though. Because the sprinklers destroyed a lot of the books in the library. Including all of the Star Wars graphic novels.

Maybe I could have done something to save them, if I had known.

00:15:01

ALICE

How can Hogan think Noah is the second shooter? Noah? It's too ridiculous to even contemplate. So ridiculous that I can't stop myself from venting even more as I stand over him.

"My brother—who cannot even tie his own shoes—somehow masterminded this crazy plan to bring a gun to school and shoot out display cases . . . and set off explosives . . ."

I glare at Hogan. But he's not going to sit there and get yelled at—not even by me. He rises to his full six feet and towers over me.

Isabelle gets between us—though it isn't quite clear who she's protecting.

Maybe Hogan is laying blame because he really is involved somehow. I didn't think so when Isabelle was questioning him. But now, I'm not so sure. After all, he is a thug, a disgruntled student being forced to perform in a pep rally he'd rather avoid. And he does have anger issues. Who knows? Maybe Hogan did have a whole other show in mind. It's possible. And he was in the hallway right before the explosion went off in the main stairwell.

I poke his furry chest. "For all I know, you tossed that bomb in the stairwell!"

Hogan stares me down. "For all I know, you did. You're the one out sneaking around the halls during a lockdown." He turns to Isabelle. "And you're the one completely losing it." He groans, and rubs his hands through his hair in frustration. "This is stupid. What even makes you think there is an accomplice?"

"Bri," Isabelle says. "The security cameras caught someone else running from the atrium."

"So, let's say there is some second shooter," Hogan says. "What makes you so sure it's me—or even a guy?"

Okay, maybe we are jumping to conclusions. I have to agree with him on that—at least until he says what he says next.

"You're acting hysterical. Both of you. Typical. Let me guess—you've got your periods, right?"

So much for facts and rational thinking.

"Oh you did NOT just say that!" Izzy retorts in her melodramatic way—one that only seems to further support Hogan's ridiculous theory. "What is it with you guys? Blame PMS. Yeah, that must be it, because it can't possibly be the idiot males that are driving us crazy!"

"I'm just saying," Hogan yells over her, "I could as easily accuse one of you. C'mon, Iz, you're no poster child for mental health." He swings his hands up to make air quotes and accidentally knocks the phone from her hand.

"Watch—" she shouts, and fumbles, but the phone falls and hits the floor. Isabelle bends and picks it up, cursing when she sees the shattered screen. "Great, just great."

I take a deep breath. "Look," I say, trying to calm everyone down, for Noah's sake as much my own. He's ramping up again.

"Things are getting out of hand. We don't have proof. It could have been some guy—"

"Or girl," Hogan cuts in.

"Or girl," I continue, "just running away from the danger. We don't even know for sure that there IS a second shooter—"

"Oh, there is." Xander is still sitting on the ground, and his monotone can be heard from behind the camera lens.

"Wait . . . what?" I turn to him. We all do. "What are you saying?"

"There are two shooters, and I can prove it." He presses the button and takes one last picture. Then he lowers his camera to reach in his backpack. We stare at him expectantly.

Maybe he has a photo of this mysterious second shooter. If anyone saw Maxwell Steinberg's accomplice, Xander did. He sees everything, or so it seems. But as he pulls his hand out of the bag, it isn't holding a photo, or a box, or even another camera.

Just a gun. A black one, like the ones in Max's photo. Xander holds it at arm's length, pointing it right at us. He closes one eye. And, finger on the trigger, Xander squeezes.

Click.

HOGAN

I am on him seconds after I see the gun. My body reacts even before my brain registers.

BANG!

The shot rings out against the cement walls and it hits me—right in the chest—as I dive in front of the girls. I land face down with a thud. The tile cold and hard against my cheek.

So this is it, I think. This is how I die. On a bathroom floor. Just like Randy.

I've pictured it a million times since Randy died. Imagined myself dead a thousand ways. Accidents. Illnesses. Even suicide. Only I never did anything about it.

Didn't even have the balls to do that, eh, Hulkster?

But it's done now.

Only . . .

Only, I don't want it.

I don't want to die.

I fight for a breath but it isn't coming. Panic washes over me as I gasp.

Is this how it felt, Randy?

"Hogan!" Alice rolls me over onto my back and I look up at the stain on the ceiling tiles. The air vent. The glow around the lights. My chest aches. Alice puts her hand on it, but it won't help. I'm sure my heart is bleeding out.

But she doesn't get Izzy to call 9-1-1. She doesn't start CPR, even though my breath is gone. Instead, she sits back and sighs.

"Holy, Hogan, you scared the hell out of me." Alice wipes her forehead with the back of her hand and I see yellow on her palm. On her fingers. It leaves a smear on her face.

Is that . . . is that paint?

Alice helps me sit up and I finally take a deep breath, surprised to discover that I can, surprised to see my fur is splattered with yellow, not red. The gun is on the floor. A paintball pistol. A RAP4, just like Randy and I used to use.

A toy.

I feel like an idiot. A bruised idiot. But it looked so real from the other end of the barrel.

Xander sits in his corner, hands over a gash on his forehead.

"Noah," Alice explains to me. "He hit him with his broom handle."

"It isn't real," Xander whines as he rubs his skull. "It's a paintball pistol. He didn't have to hit me." He scowls at Noah, who has retreated once again to the far corner, both hands cupping his ears, hat rolled down over his eyes.

"Shut up, Xander," Izzy says, moving to sit on the red gym bag, where she's trying to get her phone to work. Glad to see she's so concerned about me.

"I was just showing you," Xander continues. "You asked who the shooter was." He touches his scalp, examines his fingertips. "I'm bleeding! He made me bleed!"

"I'll show you bleeding." I get up and grab Xander by the throat. I feel my blood pulsing through my body as I slam his head against the metal stall. "You can't just go around pointing guns at people, shooting people." Slam! I push him again. Slam! "Even if it is a paintball gun, you moron."

Alice grabs my arm and I let go and Xander sinks to the floor. What I really want to do is beat the snot out of him for scaring the girls. The entire school, really. And yes, I admit, for scaring the crap out of me.

"I know. I know." Xander coughs. "That's what I told him."

"Who?" Alice asks. "Maxwell?"

Xander nods.

"What else do you know?" she says, but her voice isn't accusing. And I realize, then, what she's on to. This guy knows all about Maxwell Steinberg and his psycho plans. If anyone can protect us, all the kids at St. F.X., ironically, it's Xander.

He looks at us, at me and Izzy and Alice and even Noah, like he's thinking about whether or not he should say it. I move to grab him by the throat again, ready to squeeze it out of him, but Alice cuts in front. Her boldness shocks me. For all she knows, he does have another gun, a real one, in that bag of his. But if she's concerned about the gun on the floor or the one that might be in his bag, she doesn't show it. Instead, she squats down in front of him. Smiles, like she does, with her eyes. Speaks in her gentle voice.

"It's okay, Xander," she says, softly. "It's going to be okay. Just tell us. Tell us all of it."

ISABELLE

He's got to be kidding me. "You've been sitting there the whole time," I blurt from across the room, trying to stay as far away from him as possible, "the whole time . . . and you never told us anything about what you know?"

Xander blinks. "You didn't ask."

"Well, we're asking you now, geek," Hogan says, his tone a language all its own. One Xander obviously doesn't speak, because he continues to just sit there, blinking at us like he doesn't know what the question is.

"It might help," Alice says, like she's a translator or something, "if you ask him something specific."

"What is this guy Maxwell up to?" I say.

"What do you numbnuts have planned?" Hogan squats down and pokes him with his thick finger.

I think of the explosions I heard in the hall. "Is he going to blow up the school?" I look at the paint gun. "Or shoot us as we leave? Or what?"

Who knows what crazy things this guy has come up with.

Xander looks at the floor, trying to avoid Hogan, which is kind of hard considering he pulled him back up to standing and is right up in his face. "I don't know . . . he wasn't supposed to . . . I thought it was—"

"Well?" Hogan snaps.

Xander stalls. Like how my phone does if I've opened too many apps at once.

"Give him a second," Alice says. "Let him think."

Whose side is she on, anyway? Let him think? What is there to think about? Either he's in on it or he isn't. Why waste time waiting for him to come up with more lies?

"Do you have any more guns?" Hogan pokes him again.

"No, just the—"

"Do you want to hurt us?" I'm still trying to make sense of this whole crazy thing. Is it a prank? Or are we in real danger here?

"No!" Xander looks up in surprise, like I've said something crazy. "Why would I want to—?"

"Hello?" I snap. "You brought a gun to school. What? Is it for, like, show-and-tell?"

Hogan picks up the pistol and drops it in the sink out of Xander's reach.

"It was a mission," Xander says, like that means anything. "I didn't mean for anyone to get hurt, I—"

"This isn't some stupid game," Hogan says, getting up in his face again.

"What happens next?" I ask. If anyone knows something, it's got to be him. "This is serious, Xander. You're, like, messing with people's lives here!"

Xander looks panicked. He should. Maybe he's finally getting how big of a deal this is.

"Well?!" Hogan yells, throwing up his arms like some big hairy gorilla. "Spit it out!" I half expect him to start pounding his chest like King Kong. But seriously, Xander's driving us all nuts.

"Stop!" Alice yells, and she gets between Xander and Hogan. All one hundred pounds of her. She puts her hand on Hogan's chest, like that's going to stop him. "You have to let him think! Give him time to answer," she says, sternly. And, surprisingly, Hogan steps off.

Xander slumps to the ground and takes a few deep breaths as Alice moves to sit cross-legged in front of him. Close, but not touching. What is she waiting for? Xander is the key to getting all our answers. About Maxwell. About the shooting. About how the heck we can end this thing. Xander clenches his jaw. Stares at the floor. He seems as confused and scared as we are.

Finally she speaks, soft and steady. "This wasn't the plan, was it?"

Xander glances up at her with a look of relief. Like someone actually gets it. "No. This was not the plan. Not at all."

"What was supposed to happen?" she asks gently.

Xander takes another deep breath. "Our next mission."

"Jumping on the bandwagon?" I snort. "That's original."

No one knows who the original guys are. Lots of kids bragged about copycatting those X-morons with pranks of all sizes. Some copycats got caught, thankfully, but I heard that the original X-Men never were. And that they were planning something big for the year end. Just what I needed. Some geeked-out idiots wrecking prom.

Alice glances at the yearbook cover. The red X in a circle. The yellow paint on her fingers.

"The X-Men characters . . . they're from comics, right?" she asks.

I want to yell at her to focus. Seriously. Now is not the time to chitchat about his stupid hobby.

"Xavier and Magneto," he says, reaching for his encyclopedia. He shows her a picture of two characters: some bald guy in a wheelchair and another one in a helmet and cape. Just like those dumb doodles on every boys' bathroom door.

"Alice," I say, "we don't have time—"

She holds up her hand, as if shutting me up. I kid you not.

"X-Men," she says, to Xander. "Kind of like you guys—you and Maxwell?"

"And the rugby team," I mutter, crossing my arms, "and about a dozen other wannabes."

"But you started it," Alice says, completely ignoring me. "You and Max. You guys are the original X-Men?"

Xander nods, smiles faintly.

Wait . . . what? That's not possible. Maxwell? And this guy? These are the masterminding pranksters that have been making my life a living hell? He can't even finish a sentence.

Hogan leans in, interested now. "So the ping pong balls, the skeleton, the plane, the streaking, all those pranks—that was you?" He almost seems impressed. Shocked, actually.

Xander nods. "Well, it was mainly Max. He did it. I just took the pictures and kept a log." Xander shuffles through the photos once again and pulls out a bunch. Max with his arm around the skeleton. Max wearing nothing but his cape and helmet. Max holding a bag of ping pong balls. Max and a foil penis. Max shooting paintballs at the grad mural.

Alice almost loses it when she sees that one. "I spent weeks—" She clenches her jaw.

"So you prank people, whatever." Hogan picks up the gun photo once more. "But is this lockdown just another stunt?"

"I thought it was," Xander admits. "My job was to hit the security cameras with paint pellets. But when Max started shooting out the display cases, and I saw smoking holes in the walls where there should have been paint splatters, I realized that Max's gun was real." He looks down, ashamed. "And that's when I ran."

I can't tell if he's embarrassed by the prank or the fact that he ran away.

"Wait," I say. "Why the display cases? It seems kinda lame compared to all the other things you did."

The tips of his ears redden. "Max did that for me. He told me he'd find a way to get back at Mr. Strickland for kicking me out of Yearbook. For never putting my pictures on display. Max said they were good enough to hang in a gallery." For a second, he looks almost proud. "He said that my pictures, the ones of him, especially the ones from today's mission, would be famous."

"If you call 'on the six o'clock news' famous," Hogan mutters.

So, it was part of Max's plan to not only do these things, but to keep a record. To be infamous. My stomach twists. This changes things, because it means this mission is much more than just another prank. I look at Hogan. And Alice. They know it too.

Alice leans in a bit closer. "Can you tell us anything about Max's plan?"

Xander frowns.

Clearly he can't. Or won't.

I lift my phone. Enough of this messing around. Obviously the cops didn't hear that shot and aren't coming to save us. I'm not talking to Bri, but in this case, I'll make another exception. I need her to tell the cops what we know.

"We should let the police deal with this. That's their job, right? Let them ask the questions." I press the start button a few times but the screen stays black. I groan. Mom's gonna kill me. This is my third one this semester. "Nice, Hogan. You broke my phone. It's dead."

"Don't blame me," he says. "You're the one throwing it around."

I roll my eyes.

"Don't worry. I'm sure your parents will replace it." His tone makes it sound like an insult.

Yes, they probably will. After a long lecture. But doesn't Hogan get it? Don't any of them understand? That phone is our only link to the outside world. That phone is our only chance of passing on what we've figured out about this whole mess. About Xander. And

Max. The police might know his name, but not what we know. One text from me would make all the difference.

"I don't suppose any one of you guys have your cell . . . or your flip phone on you?" I say, knowing the answer even as I ask.

Ugh! Of all the people to be locked up with.

XANDER

I thought Max would be mad when he found the blue 120-page notebook in my backpack, when he read my journal, when he saw that I'd been writing Mission Logs. I told him that I have to write things down, like how my Social Autopsies help me figure stuff out. I was terrified that he would not invite me on any more missions. But he wasn't mad. In fact, he was excited. Said it was a great idea because, "How else will they get how amazing we are?"

I don't know who they are. But I sure like hearing Max say that we're amazing. I sure think he is. Like, capital-A Amazing. Max is a genius, I think. Or very close to it. His mind, like mine, doesn't work like anyone else's. Only, unlike me, Max never apologizes for being different. Just like how Magneto never apologizes for being Magneto.

The other thing I noticed about Max is that he is always watching. I need the Tank, and chemicals, and lots of time to develop what Max sees and knows instantly. "Opportunities"— that's what he calls them—a moment to make a difference. Max sees those all the time. Sometimes they look like bad choices, because they are technically against the rules, like breaking into the school at night, or making our own grad mural, or when he blew up a whole garbage can full of ping pong balls during an assembly. That one was my favorite. Though I wasn't too fond of having to spend hours the night before painting a red X on every ball. Mom is still wondering where her red nail polish went.

But Max has vision. He sees the hidden opportunities that everyone else misses. Like fire drills. And rugby games.

Lots of people were saying the X-Men missions were done by the rugby team—even some of the players started bragging. So, right as the St. F.X. team started to play, this guy came running across the field wearing a purple cape, red Chuck Taylor All Stars, a red metal helmet—and nothing else. All the fans cheered and screamed as he streaked through the game. I knew it was Magneto because of the helmet (worn to protect against telepathic attacks). And I knew it was Max, because that helmet had gone missing from the display shelf in Comic Corner after his shift the day before. I took seventeen pictures as he crossed the field with Coach Dufour and three players in pursuit. Then he jumped the fence and disappeared, but the crowd cheered on.

Max proved three things that day:

1. The rugby players had nothing to do with the X-Men missions.

2. Magneto totally rules!
3. Max is faster than their fastest players. HE should get MVP.

But mostly, it proved what I concluded long ago: Max is brilliant. I never saw that opportunity. It would never have occurred to me to streak across the field. But Max saw it and took it. He is a mastermind.

I wish I could know what Max is thinking, what he's planning next, but no one knows how his unique mind works. And Max doesn't even need Magneto's helmet to keep people out of his head.

So when Mr. Wilson called an assembly two weeks ago and told the whole school that, effective immediately, these pranks would stop or there would be serious consequences—no more sports, no more dances, no more intramurals, or even prom—I wondered if that was the end of our Prank Fridays. Maybe Operation Lightning Streak truly was our last mission. Mr. Wilson demanded names. But no one spoke. No one knew—except for me and Max. My face burned and I couldn't sit still. What if Mr. Wilson found out? What would happen to us?

But no one said anything, and eventually Mr. Wilson sent us back to class. As we filed out of the cafetorium that day, all the kids were grumbling—but not about Wilson. They were complaining about us!

Screw these X-Men!

Seriously—they're such idiots.

It's not our fault they're doing all these dumb pranks.

My scholarship depends on placing at the track meet. What if it's canceled?

He wouldn't cancel prom—not for real, right?

Brotherhood of Morons

. . . so immature . . .

This is my future they're messing with now, stupid losers.

Someone should turn them in.

212

Anyone know who they are?

I didn't see or hear from Max for a few days. I thought maybe he'd given up on our missions. But not Max. Like I said, he has vision.

He came into Comic Corner on my next shift and he was angry. He blamed Principal Wilson for trying to turn all those fickle humans against him. His eyes were hot, intense, like lasers burning into mine. I wanted to look away. To tell him that maybe we should lie low for a while.

He told me there's a war coming and asked me if I was sure I was on the right side, quoting it right from the movie we'd seen a hundred times. I knew he had something planned. Something big.

"You in?" he asked. "You loyal to the Brotherhood?"

I swallowed. Gave one, slow nod. I never even blinked. He gave me a list: ping pong balls, electrician's tape, chemicals, ball bearings, batteries—all kinds of random stuff I could get from Home Depot. I asked if we were doing another ping pong blast.

"Bigger," he said. "Badder. Operation Resolution. And, trust me, it's gonna blow their little minds."

00:11:07

ALICE

In my gut, I know Xander didn't mean to hurt anyone. Not even Hogan. I glance at Hogan standing protectively just over my shoulder, and blush at the thought that someone is looking out for me. Even if I don't need it.

Xander's eyes widen at Isabelle's mention of calling the police. He bites his lip. I can feel him withdrawing into himself at the thought.

Just as well we can't call them. Not yet. They won't get any answers, not from him. They won't even know what to ask, or how. He'd shut down completely. No, it has to be here. Now. I have to find out whatever I can first, and then tell it to the police. They don't need Xander, really. They need information.

And it seems that only I speak his language. Only I know how to get it.

"What did Max ask you to do to help get ready for today?" I

say. The more literal and specific the question, the easier it is for him to answer.

Xander repeats his shopping list—electrician's tape, wire, ball bearings, ping pong balls.

Hogan says it sounds like the items for the ping pong ball prank. "Maybe he's doing that one again."

But why? If anything, Maxwell Steinberg is smart. Innovative. He won't repeat a past prank any more than an author would rehash a scene. The pranks are like plot points in a story. Each one has to be new and exciting, bigger and better than the last. Each one has to raise the stakes.

"All that effort, just to repeat the ping pong thing?" I shake my head. "It just doesn't make sense."

Hogan shrugs. "We're talking about a nobody whose sole purpose is to play practical jokes on his school. Clearly, this guy doesn't have a whole lot of sense."

"Oh, he does," Xander says, enthusiastically. "Max is a mastermind."

I chew on the ends of my hair. I'm missing something. But what?

"You mentioned that you kept a log?" I ask.

Xander rummages in the backpack and pulls out a blue note-book with superhero scribbles and stickers all over the front. He pauses, holds it to his chest, as though unsure if he wants it shared.

"Dude, I'm not interested in reading your Dear Diary crap." Hogan snatches it and flips to the last entry. "All I care about is what Maxwell said about today."

"He called his last mission 'Resolution,'" Xander says. "But I've only listed the ingredients. I never write about the mission until it's over. Technically, a log is for logging the details after—"

"Wait," Isabelle says, as though she's had an epiphany. "Did you say the last mission? So, today is it?"

She seems almost relieved, as though, after this last prank, her problems will be over.

She sits on the red bag and crosses her long legs in front of her as she continues, "I just thought this Magnerdo—"

"Magneto," Xander corrects her.

She rolls her eyes. "Mag-NEAT-o would've saved his big prank," she puts air quotes around it, "for the prom next month. I've been totally stressing over it ever since these dumb stunts started. And then, when Wilson said he'd cancel everything if there were any more pranks, well, I thought for sure, these X-Men would target prom for their grand finale."

"Max said people would expect it at prom." Xander seems proud that Isabelle has proved him right.

"Well, I'm just glad you're not."

Isabelle starts complaining about how much work it takes to plan a prom and how selfish it would have been to prank it. As she rambles on, Hogan scans the list of materials again.

"Matches, ping pong balls, black powder. Typical noisemaker stuff." He looks up. "Cherry bombs?"

Xander nods.

"That must have been what we heard in the stairwells," Hogan continues. "Loud but not all that dangerous."

I don't know anything about them, really. How destructive are they? How dangerous? Maybe a garbage can full of them might cause some damage?

"How many does he have?"

"Just a few," Xander says. He looks at Isabelle. "The rest are in my gym bag."

"What?" Isabelle jumps up like she's been jolted by a live wire. "You brought . . ." She backs up as far away as she can from the suddenly ominous red gym bag. "You let me . . . you mean, I've been sitting on . . . on bombs? Ohmigod! OH. MY. GOD."

"Well, they're not lit," Xander says, as though she is being ridiculous. For once, I don't think she is. She's always so overly dramatic, but sitting on a bag of explosives, especially ones made by Xander and Maxwell—to be fair, that truly warrants a big reaction.

"Randy and I made some and shot them off in the backwoods," Hogan says to Xander. "Nearly blew my hand off. They aren't as safe as you'd think." He looks back at the list. "But this other stuff, ball bearings . . . these chemicals . . . what's this for?"

Xander looks down. Fiddles with his laces. "Max was working on some Special Project. I got the stuff, just like he asked. But he wouldn't let me help. He said it was top secret." Clearly, being left out of the plans upsets him. "But I don't know what he made."

Hogan looks at me, as if for confirmation. I nod. "He's telling the truth," I say, sure of it. "He doesn't know any more than that." Xander doesn't lie. I don't really know him, other than the readings he's done in Writer's Craft. X-Men adventures, superhero stuff. I wish I'd paid closer attention. But I do know a few things. For one, he is factual. And literal. And brutally honest. He showed that many times when giving other kids feedback. He has no filter.

Isabelle raises an eyebrow. "So, how did you pay for all the stuff?"

"My mom's credit card," Xander mumbles.

"Totally traceable." She sighs. "Sounds to me like he used you to get what he wanted: pictures of himself, supplies, a scapegoat." Isabelle glances at the sack of ping pong bombs on the far side of the room. "So, basically, he pulls the prank of the year and you're left, literally, holding the bag. Nice. I thought you were friends."

Xander looks away.

"So, why ball bearings?" I ask. They seem pretty specific.

Xander looks up. "I figured that had something to do with Magneto." He pulls a little silver ball from his jeans front pocket and holds it between his finger and thumb. "The real Magneto can manipulate magnetic fields and control metals, and in *X2: X-Men United* he escapes from his plastic prison using—"

"Small metal balls," Hogan finishes, his voice serious. "Yeah. I saw the movie."

"But in the original comic version—"

"Come on," Isabelle snorts, cutting Xander off. "He's playing a role. Maxwell is not the real Magneto," she says. "I mean, how much harm can he do with a few—?"

"Not a few—549 ball bearings." Xander holds up the little ball. "I kept one."

"Okay, 549 little silver balls?" she says, dismissively. "What— is he spilling them in the halls to make us trip?"

I take the ball bearing from Xander. Roll it in my palm. Hold it between my fingers.

"It's a tiny ball of metal," Isabelle mocks.

"Right," I say, as it dawns on me. I swallow. "And so is a bullet."

No one speaks.

"What? So you think he's firing them from his paintball gun?" Isabelle asks.

"No." Xander takes back the ball, considers it. "We tried that a few weeks ago. They don't have much trajectory. Not enough for impact. And today he had a real gun. If he wanted to shoot anyone, he'd use that." He looks up at us and, realizing what he's just said, quickly adds, "Not that he wants to shoot anyone. At least, I don't think he does. He never said . . ."

Hogan squats by the bag and unzips it. "There's got to be something else in here . . . some kind of clue." He gingerly shifts the stuffed ping pong balls, careful not to upset them. I wish he'd just leave it alone altogether. If he nearly blew his hand off with just one, what will a whole bagful do in a small room like this?

"Chain link, locks . . . and . . ." Hogan pulls out a spiral note-book, "this."

I move next to him as he opens it. Blue ballpoint-pen doodles cover the paper, fill the margins. Page after page of them.

Isabelle peeks over. "More dumb comic stuff. Does every guy go through that phase? Is it, like, a puberty thing?"

But these aren't just doodles. The drawings have an energy about them. The lines are bold. Intense. In some places the explosions he scribbled were etched into the pages until they ripped. I run my fingers along the paper, feeling the braille of the drama from the flip side.

"Is this yours?" I ask Xander. He shakes his head and comes over to join us. All of us are drawn to the notebook like rubber-neckers at a car accident.

And it is like a car accident. Random. Crazy. Messy. Page after page after page of bizarre comic spreads where some caped, masked superhero shoots jagged thunderbolts, laser beams, or dotted lines that all end in big, exploding stars.

"It's like some effed-up Where's Waldo?" Hogan says, turning the page to the same story, different setting. "There he is . . ." He turns the page. "There he is." Turn. "There he is." With every flip, the caped character becomes easier to find, usually levitating over all the carnage.

"Looks like Max wastes a lot of time in class," Isabelle says.

"Well," Hogan adds, "I doubt he'll be getting hired by Marvel any time soon."

"Seriously," Isabelle agrees. "Like, obsess much?"

"Wait! Wait!" I shout. "Go back!"

Hogan pauses and flips back one page.

And I see my Tree of Knowledge mural, or a crude rendition of its swirling branches and oval leaves. Half of the tree, anyway. The other half is buried under a vicious scribble shooting out from the caped man's gun. In this version it's a flamethrower. I grab the notebook from Hogan and flip back through what we've seen. And suddenly it clicks.

The mural.

The garbage can.

The airplane.

The sprinklers.

The skeleton.

"These aren't doodles or random comics," I say, breathless as I flip back to the beginning, to where a lewd skeleton smokes a cigarette. I look up at the three faces near mine. "Do you know what these are?"

"A waste of time?" Hogan says.

"A geek's fantasy?" Isabelle adds.

"Better," I grin. "These are blueprints. Don't you get it? These are plans, outlines for every X-Men prank. And if we know what he's planning . . ."

Hogan smiles back. "Then we know how to stop him."

HOGAN

Alice flips through the pages. "Look, see? There's the ping pong one. Books and sprinklers—that's the library. This one has a toilet . . ." She looks up.

"Mr. Wilson's washroom," Xander says. "Not a lot of people knew about that one. Operation Fire-in-the-Hole. Once everyone cleared out for the fire alarm, we climbed through the ceiling into the washroom Wilson keeps locked and rigged his toilet with some sodium. It explodes when water contacts it. I bet it made a huge mess."

I look at the picture and see it now. A toilet exploding as some guy, probably Wilson, flies bare-assed over the moon.

I smile at Alice, amazed that she somehow figured out how to see the story in the scribbles.

Xander stares wide-eyed at the book. Then he grabs it from Alice and continues flipping, searching for something, growing more and more agitated with every page turn.

"Haven't you seen this book before?" I say. "I just took it from your bag."

Xander keeps flipping. "It's Max's bag. I grabbed it before I left the atrium. I thought maybe he would abort the mission if he didn't have all his stuff."

"Try the last pages—the blueprint for Resolution is probably there," Alice suggests. But Xander stops flipping and lowers his hands.

"Missing," he says, so quietly I almost think I imagined it.

Alice takes it from him and keeps searching. "What?" she asks. "Resolution?"

"No. His partner," Xander says. He looks like he's gonna cry. "I was with him on every mission and he never drew me once. Not even as a sidekick. Not in any of them."

"Be thankful," Izzy says. "The last place you wanna be is in some psycho's journal."

"But Isabelle . . ." Alice says, her voice sounding serious. "You're in this picture." She spreads the book wide open before Isabelle, the pages trembling in her hands.

I find Where's Weirdo? easily in all the explosions, rain, and thunderbolts. But this drawing is different. The ground isn't ground exactly, but arms, legs, severed heads with Xs for eyes. Pieces in puddles. Each of them named. And with a shaky finger, Alice points to the one marked "Isabelle Parks."

Izzy whimpers beside me. "Why would he . . .? I don't even . . . I never . . ."

I try to reassure her. "It's not just you, Iz. There's about fifty names. And that one there with the W, the guy from the toilet, he's in all the pictures. Probably Wilson."

"But I don't even know him," Izzy's voice pleads. "Why would he target me?"

I shrug. "School president?"

"This is it," Alice says, anxiously. "Resolution. This is what Maxwell is planning for today." She bends down and lays the book open on the floor. We all kneel around it trying to make sense of the scribbles.

At the center of the drawing hangs some kind of ball with light or lasers shooting from it in all directions.

"Disco ball?" Izzy says. "No, Disco Day was last month during Spirit Week. Are you sure this is the right page?"

But then I look at the lines coming out of the ball, at the circles at the other end. I've seen something like this before. "Wait a second." I flip back a few pages to a diagram of a garbage can and a load of ping pong balls. It dawns on me then. The explosion. The ball bearings. "It's not a disco ball—it's a bomb."

"Like one of those cherry things . . . but bigger?" Alice asks.

I wish it was. But that sinking feeling in my stomach tells me I'm onto something. "Remember the ping pong explosion?" I point at the picture. The garbage can surrounded by dashes and dots. I flip back to Resolution. "Well, picture that, but bigger. Way bigger. With ball bearings instead of ping pong balls."

Alice's eyes go wide. "With enough force, it would be like firing hundreds of bullets in all directions, all at once."

We look down at the picture and see exactly that.

"Could he really build something like that?" Izzy asks, skeptically.

"Max can build anything," Xander says.

"So we know what. But where?" Alice asks. "When? And how is he going to trigger it?"

Xander shrugs. "He didn't tell me."

We sit for a minute staring at the drawings, each of us hoping we'll see some other clue. But nothing comes.

Alice chews on the ends of her hair as she stares through the pages, deep in thought. "If I were Maxwell, I'd want to set this off where I get the biggest impact, right? The most damage."

"Well, apparently he's already destroyed our trophy case," Izzy says.

"Yes . . ." Alice says, "but it's not about damaging property."

Her comment hangs heavy between us. I wonder if that's it. If Maxwell was planning to cross that line. Pranks are funny, yeah, but the thing is, once you do one, you raise the bar. And with everyone copycatting his little pranks, the next has to be even bigger, even better, even crazier.

How insane is this guy?

I think of the photo. The eyes.

Crazy enough.

"Hello?" Izzy chirps. "We've been in a lockdown for over forty-five minutes, hidden away in locked classrooms. How would he get at us even if he wanted to?"

"Think about it," Alice says, her eyes almost as intense as Max's. "Where are there no cameras—thanks to Xander? Where can he set up this next prank without being seen? Just like their fire alarm Fridays. And where will crowds of people go when the lockdown ends?"

She's kinda freaking me out right now. But I wonder if she's onto something.

Izzy's mouth drops open. She whispers, "The atrium."

It makes sense. All except the lockdown part. "The lockdown won't end until they catch Maxwell," I say.

And just then, the fire alarm goes off.

NOAH

Fire Drill Social Story

When the FIRE ALARM sounds

the kids leave the classroom go outside through EXIT A

to line up for attendance in the BACK FIELD.

CLANG! CLANG! CLANG!

Stop!
Roll down the dark
But it keeps CLANG-CLANG-CLANGING-ING-ING-ING
ING my ears, ING my eyes, ING my head.
Exploding sounds and colors.
No matter how I hit.

". . . just a fire alarm!"

Alice's voice sounds so far away.
Why won't she get me?
Why won't she make it stop?

Fire alarm?

No.No.No.No.
This isn't right.
Exit A. Exit A.
The field.
The field.
Kim is waiting for me at the back field.

ALICE

Everyone cowers and covers their ears at the piercing ring of the fire alarm. My heart thuds in my chest. The bell continues its clanging as I crawl over to Noah, who shrieks and punches at his head trying to make it all stop.

"What do we do?" Isabelle yells.

"We just ignore it, right?" Hogan suggests. "Isn't that the rule?"

"Unless you smell something burning," Isabelle adds.

"Yes . . . but . . . maybe it's a trick," I say. "If we're right about the blueprint, he wants us to gather in the atrium."

"Or maybe he really has set the school on fire." Isabelle eyes the bag of cherry bombs.

A tendril of smoke snakes its way under the wooden door, then disappears out the window. It's just your imagination. Your overactive imagination. It's not real. Terrified, I look at Hogan. I can tell by his expression he saw the smoke too.

"That's it!" he says, heading for the door. "If it's a trap, we have to warn everyone. And if it's not, we can't stay here. We're getting the hell out! Now!"

He slams his fists against the metal door he wedged in to keep Maxwell out. Stuck like a tabletop between the wooden door and the side of the pedestal sink, it doesn't budge. He lifts his foot and slams it hard. Two, three times.

A tremor of realization ripples through me—what kept us safe might keep us trapped. Might cost our lives.

Undeterred, Hogan pummels with his fists like a boxer with a bag. He pounds at the door for what feels like forever as we stand and watch him grow redder, angrier, sweatier, his knuckles red raw, bruised, and bloodied from the metal. Then, breathless, he stops and unzips the mascot costume, shedding his second skin and dumping it in a heap on the floor. Flexed and sweaty, in nothing but his purple boxers, he looks like the Incredible Hulk himself, his thick fists smashing left and right and left and right. The metal dents but doesn't move. Hogan tries kicking it. Kneeing it. Wrenching it. Tries everything he can to get it out. To get us out.

"There's always the cherry bombs." Xander kneels by the bag. "We could blast it—"

"NO!" Isabelle and I shout in unison.

"Soak them in the sink," Hogan orders. And Xander does. He saturates every one of them. The last thing we need in a fire is to be gathered around a powder keg.

More smoke seeps through the cracks. There is no rationalizing it away. Something is burning outside this room.

The smoke, the yelling, the clang-clang-clang of that damn alarm—all of it is too much for Noah who, hat over his face, furiously slams his head over and over and over in a vain attempt to make it all stop. For a moment, I feel as though all of our efforts are just as futile. We are all freaking out in our own ways: me trying to swaddle my brother in Hogan's abandoned fur; Isabelle back to turning her phone on and off and on and off in the hopes that it might miraculously reboot; Hogan hammering at a jammed metal door that won't budge; Xander in a panic as he rummages through the wet bag. It just seems so hopeless.

"What are you looking for, Xander?" I yell over the piercing alarm and the thunder of Hogan's pummeling.

"The trigger," he says. "A detonation would need some kind of detonator." He digs around a bit and then slumps back on his heels. "Nothing."

"Maybe it's the same trigger as the ping pong one," Isabelle says, looking up from her phone.

"No." Xander checks the side pockets. "That was liquid nitrogen. Enough to blast light balls out of an open garbage can, but not enough to shoot metal. Well, not with enough velocity to pierce skin."

Isabelle blanches, no doubt recalling the comic version of herself in Max's book.

The pounding stops. Breathless, Hogan bends over and drops to one knee. Sweat runs down his face and he wipes it on his slick biceps. He looks defeated. No, worse than that. Crushed.

"I can't . . ." he heaves, his reddened eyes watery from the sting of smoke. "I should never have . . ."

I leave Noah for a moment and go to him. "Let me help."

It seems a ridiculous offer. As if someone as strong as Hogan would ever want my help. "All of us." I wave everyone over. "Maybe . . . maybe if we all push together, this stupid thing will give."

Setting down their camera and phone, Xander and Isabelle join me next to Hogan, our hands gripping the edge of the dented metal.

"On three," Hogan says, and on his cue we grit our teeth and shove upwards. The door shifts forward a fraction and sticks again.

"What about Noah?" Hogan asks.

I am not sure. Noah is really agitated, but before I can say no, Hogan slips Noah's arms in the sleeves of the fisher costume and

231

eventually coaxes him over. "Push hard, Noah," he says. "We're going to open the door and we need your help, okay?"

Mimicking us, Noah takes his hands away from his ears long enough to grip the edge while Hogan squats below, wedging himself underneath the metal door. He counts, and on three we all push again, shoving upwards with all we have left. This has to work. It has to. Shouldering the metal, Hogan drives his legs, roaring and red-faced with the force of his thrust. The door moves an inch. Then gives a little more.

"It's working!" I yell, just as everyone is about to quit. "Keep going!" And with another great heave, the metal screeches free.

We fling the wooden door open and tumble out into the hall. There isn't a lot of smoke, but what there is snakes down the hallway, sucked towards the open bathroom window. Xander runs back inside and returns wearing his camera.

"This way!" Isabelle says, grabbing my arm and pulling me towards the nearest exit. It's the route we always take during drills in Ms. Carter's class. Back stairs. Down three floors. Exit to the back field. Simple enough. But when we reach the door and she shoves on the handle, it jams.

"Let me try," Hogan says, ramming it with his shoulder. He lifts his foot and slams it against the handles twice. "It must be locked or something."

"Forget it. Let's try the other one," Isabelle yells. There are stairs at the end of every hall, and she takes off running for the next ones with Xander close on her heels. Hogan starts forward and, after a few steps, looks back for us.

"Come on." I grab Noah's free hand. In the other, he grips his broken broom handle. There is less than a foot of it left, but I hope it gives him some comfort. Just like his furry sleeves and the cape of costume that flaps behind him as we start to run towards the source of the smoke.

ISABELLE

I hit the west stairwell doors first and press on the bar. It gives a bit, but just like the others, these doors don't open. Looking through the window, I notice something just as Xander runs past me, around the corner, and disappears into the smoky hall.

"It's chained," I say to Hogan and Alice as they arrive.

"What?!" Alice gasps.

"That must have been what we heard," Hogan says. "And there was more chain in the bag. Maxwell must have been sneaking around and chaining the doors."

The smoke is thicker here but not as bad as down the hall by the main stairs. "I don't think we should go any farther," I say. Xander ran that way, so he must be stupider than I thought. "That's heading into the fire."

"It won't matter," Alice says. "I'll bet the other stairwells are locked too."

I whimper. "Ohmigod, is that it? Is he trying to burn us alive?" My eyes sting, and I don't know if it's from smoke or fear. Noah coughs.

"The smoke is getting worse," Hogan says. I think he's right. It's not just a haze, it's a cloud gathering overhead. "So what's the plan, guys? We can't just stay here."

"Get everyone the hell out." I try a few classrooms but, of course, they are locked. "Guys!" I bang on the doors. "Forget the lockdown! There's a fire!" But they won't come out. Not even if it's me. Not until they see the smoke for themselves, and it might be too late by then.

Xander comes barreling around the corner, lost in a black cloud like he's on fire himself. I scream, and Hogan slams him to the ground and starts swatting at his clothes, trying to put him out.

"Stop! Stop!" Xander yells.

The two of them sit up, breathless, and we see he's not on fire. In fact, he's not even singed.

Alice bends over the smoking tinfoil something or other that Xander dropped as he fell. "Smoke bombs?" she says.

Hogan helps Xander to his feet.

"Yes," Xander pants. "They're in several corners. And all the corner stairwell doors are locked, just like the others."

I feel my shoulders relax a bit. "So there's no fire? That's a relief."

"It shouldn't be," Alice says. "It's all part of his plan."

We all look at her, hoping she's figured it out.

"Don't you get it?" she says. "It's just like the Friday fire drills. He clears the halls, only this time, he used a lockdown. Then, when he has everything ready, he sets off the alarms."

"But why the smoke?" Hogan asks, as the black spewing from the foil forms a dark cloud above us. "Why bother with that? He could've just pulled the alarm himself."

I see where Alice is going with this. "Because," I say, "we

wouldn't leave the rooms unless we saw smoke. This was the only way to end the lockdown other than having the principal come release us room by room."

And, as if on cue, or probably because of Xander's smoke bomb still billowing on the floor, Ms. Carter's door opens and the class heads for the far stairs. Another class joins them, the panic increasing as they realize their closest exit is blocked.

They run for the door behind us. A few girls freak out. "It's locked too!" Panic sparks and spreads like fire, as the growing crowd rushes down the main hall.

Alice nods. "He chained doors to corral everyone down the main stairwell—"

I hop on her train of thought. "Straight into the—"

"Atrium." Hogan finishes.

The panicked crowds spill from the third floor into the only open stairwell. Hands over their ears, smoke in their eyes.

"Stop! There's no fire! It's a trap!" we yell, grabbing at random students. But they are so freaked out, they just shake us off as they run past.

There's no way to stop them.

Black smoke hangs overhead like some dark brainstorm. We can't stay here.

All we can do is follow. Running scared, running full tilt towards some kind of Resolution.

Just the way Maxwell Steinberg planned.

HOGAN

"**W**e have to let Mr. Wilson know!" Izzy yells as we reach the main landing. She looks through the windows at the atrium and the main office below, where already a crowd clogs around the front doors. We join the hundreds of kids filling the stairwell. The stairs split and loop back, meeting at each landing.

"Yo, Hogan!" Trev yells at me as he comes down the far side. His expression says, What the hell? He's trying to make a joke of me in my underwear. Of this whole situation. But I can tell he's freaked out. The smoke. The lockdown. The chains. Some kids are in a full-out panic. Even more so when they see me barreling through.

"Move!" I yell, shoving them aside. "Get out of my way!"

And they try to, man, they desperately try to steer clear when they see the Hulk coming at them, sweaty, yelling, and rampaging in his boxers. But every flight is packed tight, railing to railing, as the mass moves slowly downward. They've got nowhere else to go.

"MOVE IT!" I wade downstream through the current of gawkers. My recurring nightmares—I am at school practically naked and no matter how I run, how hard I try, I get nowhere.

Izzy's following close in the wake behind me. She yells something, but I can't hear her in the screaming and ringing. I look for Alice and Noah as we round the second floor but they're lost in the crowd.

But then, I see Xander coming down on the other side behind Trev. Xander stops when we reach the landing. He yells across at me, something about an opportunity. Then he turns and cuts sideways, fighting his way through to disappear through the second-floor doors.

Where the hell is he going? For a second, I wonder if maybe he's remembered something. A clue.

Or maybe he's turned back to the dark side. Once a bad guy . . . always a bad guy. Don't kid yourself, Hulkster.

No, I'm no hero. Not even close. But I have a job to do. Find Wilson. Tell him what we know: it's not a fire; it's a bomb.

So, I shove harder through the crowd, pushing against that little voice inside that wonders if maybe we got the whole thing wrong.

Terrified that we might be right.

ALICE

The crowds tear us apart and sweep me away. From Hogan and Isabelle. From Xander. From Noah.

"Noah! NOAH!" I scream as his hand is pulled from my grasp. I see his fur arms flail a few times, and then the crowd swallows him. I push back towards the surging mob, desperate to get to where I last saw him, but the wave of bodies sweeps me along and I can't escape. My only hope is that he can't either. That he, like me, is just a bit of flotsam carried in the current.

You'll find him at the bottom. In the atrium. He's fine. He'll be fine.

I say it like a mantra. I stumble as we hit the landing but the tightly packed bodies keep me from falling. God help anyone that does—they'll be trampled for sure.

He won't fall. He's fine. He'll be fine.

I will find Noah.

Hogan and Isabelle will find Mr. Wilson and tell the police.
Someone will stop Resolution.
We have to.
Because anything else is unthinkable.

NOAH

Look, sire, the herd is on the move.
Odd.
Mufasa! Quick! Stampede in the gorge—SIMBA'S down there!

The wildebeests keep running, running, running.
Spilling into the canyon.

Zazu, help me!

Alice!
Where is Alice?
Why won't she stop the movie?
Stop! Stop!
Make it stop.
I don't like this part.

Hold on, Simba!

Skip ahead.
Skip. Skip ahead.

Make it Hakuna Matata.

But no matter how hard I hit
It plays on.

And I am caught up with the wildebeests.

XANDER

May 12, 2016
Social Autopsy #84
Event: Max's Secret

I should be writing a Mission Log, but Max told me this one was Top Secret. And since I don't really understand what just happened, I thought I'd do a Social Autopsy instead.

I gave Max all the supplies I'd got, just like he asked. He never even said thanks (and it took a long time to count 550 ball bearings at Home Depot). He wouldn't let me help him. He didn't even let me come in his garage.

"I thought we were a team," I said.

And he laughed.

"Go home, Xander," he said, like I was a little kid, when actually I am a whole grade older. "Go back to your comics."

So I did.

I don't know why Max didn't want me around. I wasn't going to tell anyone. I wouldn't spoil the Top Secret surprise. Didn't he know that?

Maybe I needed to prove it to him. Maybe I had to earn his trust, like Mrs. O'Neill says. After all, #2 on the Friendship Checklist says: friends do kind things for each other.

What would Max really like? What one thing would he most want?

Actually, I could think of two. I saw them on the poster in his garage that listed Stan Lee's top 100 comics. Max said he had read them all . . . all except for two:

- *X-Men #1*
- *The Coming of the Avengers #1*

Max said he'd never get his hands on those. They were first issues. Even John Banks didn't have copies, and Comic Corner had almost everything.

But I knew exactly where they were.

I ran all the way back to Max's house and burst into the garage through the side door. Max was soldering the Magneto helmet. All the other stuff I'd brought was spread all over his bench, along with the remote for my X-Jet. The one he'd destroyed.

I asked him why he kept the remote. He looked up at me. I didn't even need a photo to recognize his face was angry. So I handed him the paper bag.

Max gave me a dirty look, but then he looked inside it and said, "Holy crap!"

At first, I did not know if that was good or bad. "Crap" is like that.

Then he pulled out the first issues of X-Men and Avengers

and got really excited. It made me happy to see Max happy. Mrs. O'Neill was right. Again.

"You like them?" I asked, even though I knew he did. I wanted him to say it.

"Like them? This is fricken' awesome!" He slipped one out of the sleeve and started flipping through it. It's okay to do that. Just not in the store.

"They were my dad's . . . but I want you to have them."

I'd debated it all the way to Max's house. What if Dad came home? What if he wanted them? But the look on Max's face told me I'd made the right decision. It had been six years. Dad wasn't coming for the comics.

Or for me.

Max asked if I was sure, said they were worth a fortune. And I realized that even if my dad didn't want something, it didn't make it any less valuable. Or any less important to someone else. So I pointed to the poster on the wall over his workbench: "100 Comics to Read Before You Die," and I told him, "Now you can finish."

I hate leaving things incomplete. Like sandwiches. Or Lego Death Stars. Or books. No matter how much I hate something, I have to get to the end.

Max didn't say anything. He just stared at me. Like, more staring than Mrs. O'Neill would find appropriate. He seemed sad, and I wondered if I had made a mistake. Maybe he didn't want the comics. Maybe I'd just made things even worse.

I turned to go.

Max asked me if I wanted to finish. His voice sounded strange, like he had something stuck in his throat, and he said, "You with me to the end, X-Man?"

I nodded so hard I thought my head might rattle.

He picked up a red gym bag. It said "FitLife" on the side in white letters. My mom has one too. She got it free for joining the gym, and she didn't even have to go to keep it. It hangs, empty, in our hall closet. But this one was heavy. It was full of something.

"Cherry bombs, paint guns, the usual," he said as he gave it to me. Then he turned back to the workbench. "I'll be bringing our secret weapon. The Special F.X."

Our secret weapon? I couldn't believe it. We were doing it. Me and Max. Together.

"Just bring that to the atrium tomorrow at 1:15. Right at the start of period 4," he said over his shoulder as he went back to his soldering. "I'm relying on you."

I told him I would. I'd do anything he asked just to be a part of anything he did.

"We'll see, X-Man," he said, as I left him in the smoke and shadows. "We'll see."

ISABELLE

The atrium is packed with students and teachers. I don't have to hear the buzz about chains on the front doors or being trapped to know what's going on. Alice is right. This has been Maxwell's plan all along.

Hogan drives through the crowd like a snowplow. I try to keep up, but people keep pulling on my arms.

"Isabelle what's going on?"

"Isabelle, what should we . . .?"

"Isabelle, where do we . . .?"

Faceless hands grasp at me as I try to run, but can't. I lose sight of Hogan. The space is closing in behind.

"Isabelle! Izzy!" People keep calling my name. Pulling at my arms. My shoulders.

"Just stay calm!" I screech as I drive forward. I have to get to Mr. Wilson. Now. "Everyone—just STAY calm! Everything is going to be all right!"

But they don't believe me. How could they?
I don't believe it myself.

HOGAN

Wilson is standing just outside the main office. Beside him is Officer Scott, the cop assigned to our school and, unfortunately, the same cop that arrested me for stealing the bike. By the time I reach them, my heart is pounding from the effort of pushing through the crowds. I can barely catch my breath.

"Hogan?" Wilson's eyes go wide as he looks at me half-crazed and half-naked. "What the hell are you—?"

"It's not a fire!" I gasp. "It's not a prank!"

Officer Scott moves to intercept me. "Easy, Hogan. Easy."

I shrug him off and push for Wilson. He has to listen. Why won't he listen?

"Maxwell—" I gasp. "He's trying to—"

A look passes between the men, one I know all too well—suspicion. Scott grabs me, then, wrenches my arms back in some cop-hold. I could break free. Easily. But I don't.

"What do you know about Maxwell?" Scott asks.

"There's a bomb!" I say. "Maxwell is driving everyone into the atrium because that's where he's set a bomb!"

Officer Scott radios to dispatch, but he keeps a firm grip on my wrist.

Wilson gets on his walkie-talkie. "Mr. Dean, I need those bolt cutters at the front doors, NOW!" He yells to a few nearby teachers. "Mr. Miller. Get Ms. Beckman and take the students through the staff room exit."

The two teachers start herding kids two by two, like Noah's ark, through the door and hall leading to the staff room. There's no way all 1,500 of us will get through before Maxwell rains down his next surprise.

"We're running out of time!" I say.

"Just tell me, son. Tell me where it is," Wilson says to me.

I look up at the ceiling where the Doves of Peace hang from the skylight. Six huge sculptures of flying birds hang level with the second-floor windows that ring the atrium. Some art class made them as a remembrance for every student who's died since our school opened. One for Randy, too, I suppose. I'd avoided seeing it all this time.

I look away, not wanting to think about how many doves we'll need if we don't find that bomb.

I'd hoped Resolution would be more obvious. That we'd get to the atrium and see some big package on the picnic tables, some huge disco bomb just hanging there, like in his drawing. Hell, I could find Where's Weirdo? in every one of his pages. Why couldn't I see it now? Surely, he is here somewhere, too. Unless—hope sparks inside me—unless he's already been caught.

"Did the cops catch him? Maxwell?" I blurt.

"Look, Hogan." Scott moves in front of my face. He means business. "No more messing around. You are going to tell us. Right now. Where did you guys plant the bomb?"

I look away.

He thinks you're in on it. That you told him outta guilt. And that you're withholding outta shame. Ohhh yeah, Hogan! Your loser rep just keeps getting better and better!

But I don't blame them for thinking that. Why wouldn't they?

"Hogan," Wilson says, "this isn't just another prank. Not this time. We're talking life and death here." He waves his walkie-talkie at the mob of kids. "Look at them. Look!"

I scan the crowd of terrified faces. Girls crying and hugging each other. Trembling grade 7 and 8s. And Alice, like a bug-eyed grade 7 herself, lost and alone in the middle of it as she screams Noah's name.

"You don't want to see them hurt, do you?"

I shake my head. Of course not.

"Just tell me where it is," he goes, "and everything will be okay."

But it won't. Because I can't.

ALICE

"**N**oah! NOAH!" I scream until I'm hoarse. I'll never find him this way. Not in this mayhem.

I scan the wired crowd and spot Hogan talking to Mr. Wilson over on the side. At least Mr. Wilson knows now. We did our job. It's out of our hands. Finally.

But Hogan doesn't seem relieved. In fact, he looks almost defeated.

I push my way towards him. Maybe he's seen Noah. Maybe he'll help me find him. But the truth is, I just want to be near him. By him. To know that even in this crowd of hundreds, a thousand frantic people . . . we aren't alone.

The mob opens for a second, just as Officer Scott steps up in Hogan's face and Hogan slouches. In a flash, I see the whole story, read it in the slump of his shoulders. They blame Hogan. Of course they do. He is involved, but not in the way they think. He knows way more than an outsider should, so, naturally, they assume he is in on it. That he is the unknown second shooter. Heck, I even accused him of it—why wouldn't they?

I push through the crowd, eager to reach them and set things right. Hogan won't do it—not to save himself, anyway. Because, if I know anything about Hogan King, it's the story he tells himself—that he has to suffer, because he deserves it.

ISABELLE

In the thick of the crowd, I spot Hogan on the far side. He's talking to Wilson. Seconds later, the fire alarm stops and everyone cheers.

It's over. Thank God, it's over. But my stomach sinks when I see Mr. Wilson's shocked expression. He hasn't turned it off. It isn't over. Clearly, this is another part of Maxwell's plan.

"Hail Mutants!"

The voice comes over the P.A. and echoes through the atrium. I glance through the window into the office. Empty. No one is at the phone used to make our announcements.

From one of the second-floor windows a beam of light projects an image on the opposite wall. A huge head fills the space meant for our grad mural, the one we painted over—whiting out the vandalism, our way of "taking it back." With the flick of a switch, he's stolen it from us again.

A red helmet blocks most of the face, its sides cutting in like metal sideburns around his smirk and framing the eyes in a frown: Magneto. I look at the eyes, those eyes: Maxwell. Names I'd never heard until thirty minutes ago. Names I'll never forget.

Everyone turns to watch, jostles closer for a better view. Just like he hoped.

This is it. It's happening.

Only I don't know what to do but stand and watch.

The shot pulls back to show him in his purple cape, standing, hands on hips like some villain. So cliché. A bedsheet hangs behind him, painted with that damned circled red X. Some kids whistle and clap. Others heckle. They don't get it. They're so relieved to see him, to realize it's not a real fire. They just assume it's another prank.

"I have accomplished mission after mission," Max continues, "and still you doubt—no, you slander the Brotherhood! For that, you have been punished. I have locked you down. I've smoked you out," he says, raising a fist. "I am a god among insects. Do not doubt my powers."

Mr. Dean passes by me and slows to watch the video that seems to have mesmerized everyone.

"Hurry!" I shout, snapped out of my trance by the sight of two bolt cutters in his hands. I grab his second pair and push past the students towards the doors. "We're running out of time. Cut them, NOW!"

Fortunately, the video has pulled most of the crowd away from the exit. Otherwise, I doubt I'd have been to able get close enough to cut the chains. I start on one of the thick chain links looped around the handles, but it's harder than I thought. The blades bite into the dull metal and stick.

"But first," Max's voice echoes from the atrium, "let me reveal my true identity."

The crowd goes wild. Fans or not, they want to know who he is. After months of guessing names, and debating clues, all those conspiracy theorists who accused the rugby team, some dropout, rival schools, or even Mr. Boyle, the disgruntled supply teacher, now they will finally get their answer. The crowd roars and I glance back to see Maxwell remove his helmet. The roar subsides into murmuring. Clearly, they are as unimpressed as we were when we first saw Maxwell's face in the yearbook.

"Who the hell is that?" someone yells.

"That's the guy?"

"Wait . . . he's not the rugby captain."

"It just another copycat!" someone calls out.

People boo and the crowd turns. This isn't who they want. He can't possibly be the infamous Magneto, the mastermind behind all those crazy pranks. This guy? Not in a million years.

"We are all mutants, really," Maxwell's recorded voice continues. I wonder where he really is. If he hasn't already lit the fuse to the bomb, all this booing and jeering will totally push him over the edge.

I squeeze the bolt cutters' arms but I haven't the strength to make it cut through the links.

"Try the locks," Mr. Dean suggests from the far end of the doors as he snaps one loose and unravels the chain. It falls to the ground with a clank. But there are still two more locks to go. Maxwell knew what he was doing. Probably knew how long it would take to cut through three locks on each of the three sets of doors. But maybe, just maybe he didn't know there'd be two of us cutting.

A quick glance at the bottom of the video tells me time is running out. The video has thirty seconds left, if that. And I wonder if that means that's all we have, too.

"Hurry, Mr. Dean—something really bad is going to happen at the end, I just know it. We have to get everyone out!"

"Soon you humans who think you are superior will learn," Maxwell's voice says. "The hard way."

Then the screen goes black.

00:04:10

HOGAN

The video stops and something buzzes past our heads.

Wilson curses. "Not that goddammed plane again."

Only it's not a plane—this one's a drone. Four arms, each with a propeller. The flying X hovers so we can all get a good look. I remember the drawing and see the barrel of the gun duct-taped underneath. A paintgun, I think, but I can't be sure.

"Get down!" I yell, as it swoops low over the crowd, but no one listens.

A few hands grasp for it as it skims overhead. One guy even climbs up on his buddy's shoulders to catch it, eager to be the guy that took it down.

But it takes him down first.

CRACK-CRACK-CRACK!

Point blank. Three direct hits. The guy falls back into the crowd grasping at the red that splatters across his chest.

People scream.

"It's a paintball gun!" I yell, now that I know for sure. But what they see and hear tells them different. Shooting. Red smears. Hysteria.

The drone circles around for another pass and sweeps, rapid-firing as it rims the panicked crowd scrambling below. A dozen people on the outer edges cry out and fall, and the place erupts. Hundreds of them, sure they're in a war zone, rush the exits, like a manic school of fish trying to escape the shark. Some make it to the staff room door, or the front door that Mr. Dean unlocked. But the mob clogs the exits, pressing Izzy and the old janitor up against the still-chained doors, and in the madness, no one seems to be getting out.

About ten cops come running from the far hall at the sound of gunfire. They appear on the other side as Officer Scott joins with them, yelling instructions no one hears.

I grab Wilson's arm. "It's only paint." Not that it won't sting or bruise. It might even take out an eye. But it won't kill them. At least, the drone won't. But knowing Maxwell, it's just a distraction from what he's got planned next.

"Look for Maxwell!" I shout. "He's here somewhere—he has to be. That drone is remote-controlled. If we find him, maybe we can stop him."

Wilson doesn't ask how I know this or why. At this point, I'm all he's got. He nods and runs to the cops.

The crowd panics, crushing up against the picnic tables scattered throughout the atrium—nerd-feeders, I call them, because they attract a flock of geeks every spare and lunch. I hate the atrium. And not just because of the nerds, or those doves of the dead. It's the windows. Three stories of them ringing the space—it always makes me feel like I'm in a fishbowl.

Of course! The windows! What better way to watch his sick plan unfold?

I scan the glass.

Come on, Maxwell. I know you're watching. Show yourself, you coward.

But all the windows are dark. Their blinds still closed from lockdown.

All but one.

A flicker of movement catches my eye. Second floor, right above the mural. Right across from the projector.

Gotcha!

I meet Officer Scott's eyes across the atrium and point up at the room as I bolt for the stairs.

"It's him! It's Magneto!" people scream. Only they're not pointing at the second-floor window.

The crowd backs away from the empty stairwell in front of me, where a guy staggers forward, a dark shadow against the sunlight streaming in through the stairwell windows. Something on his head keeps me from seeing his face. Even his body is lost in the outline of his cloak.

Four officers burst from the crowd behind me, guns drawn.

"Stop! This is the police. Do not move!" Their voices echo in the sudden, terrified silence.

But the guy, ignoring them, takes a step and stops. Starts and stops. He slowly raises one hand.

My mind races. Maybe it is Maxwell. Maybe that second-floor shadow was Xander. Maybe the turncoat turned again.

"On the floor!" a policeman shouts, the others edging closer. "On the floor, NOW!"

But the guy doesn't listen. It's like the cops are not even there.

Maybe this final showdown is all part of Maxwell's plan. I watch his hand rise from the shadow of his cape. I know he's gripping something, even before I see it clearly.

A gun?

The trigger?

The bomb?

"Drop it!" the cop yells. "This is your last warning. DROP YOUR WEAPON!"

But the guy doesn't. He lifts that hand until it catches the light.

Everything freezes, like one of Xander's photographs, and I see it all in stark black-and-white:

the weapon—

its foot-long shaft—

a rectangle at one end.

And I bolt. I run at him full tilt. Because it isn't Maxwell or Xander. And that isn't a weapon. Or a trigger. Or a gun. Just a broken piece of broom handle, labeled with the one word I hear Alice scream as I hit him. As a gun fires—

"NOOOOOAH!"

ALICE

Hogan, running full tilt, collides with my brother just as the shot explodes, and both of them fall to the ground. Neither moves.

My God, what if . . .? What if . . .?

My mind goes numb. This is not a story I want to imagine. Not a reality I can even contemplate.

"NOAH!" I scream again. His body lies motionless in the skewed rectangle of light that spills into the atrium. The mangy fur of his cloak. The bright orange of his hat still covering his face. The dust winking in the shaft of sunlight. Numb-brained, my eyes absorb it all, record every vivid detail.

I have to get to him. To Hogan, deathly still on the other side. I elbow my way through the stunned bystanders.

Gun still drawn, an officer circles them, kicking away the weapon, and it slides towards me as I approach. The broom handle, the stupid broom handle that might have cost their lives.

Two other officers roughly roll Noah over onto his stomach, kneel on him, and wrench his arms behind his back to secure them in handcuffs. Finally, one of them yanks off Noah's hat and I start to cry.

Noah. Poor Noah, with his hair plastered to his sweaty head, his face streaked with tears, and his eyes, wide and wild in the sunlight's glare. He is terrified. More terrified than I've ever seen him.

And he is alive, thank God. He's alive. I shove my way through the crowd eager to reach him.

Another officer moves towards Hogan, kneels by him and checks his pulse. Even as he presses, I feel mine stop. He unclips his radio and requests paramedics. But through it all, Hogan never moves.

"Hogan!" I yell, veering towards him. I fall to my knees beside where he lies on his back. His eyes are closed. A hole five inches below his collarbone bubbles and oozes a dark red that puddles beside him. Blood—not paint. "Oh my God—Hogan?"

"Here." The officer takes my hand, presses it against the wound that pulses hot and slick. I want to pull away. To run away. I want to be sick. "Keep the pressure on it," he says to me. "Can you do that?"

I nod. Swallow, but my mouth is dry. "Is he going to be all—?"

"YEAAaAAARrgggh!!" Noah thrashes and snarls like a wild animal as the officers wrestle him to his feet. His face is grimaced, his neck bulging with effort.

"Stop!" I cry. "You're hurting him!" But I can't get up. I can't leave Hogan. I can't help Noah.

"Wait! No!" Isabelle pushes and shoves through the stunned crowd to Noah's side. "He's autistic; he's autistic. He doesn't understand!"

The officer seems confused. The furry suit, the hat, the dramatic entrance. Surely, this guy is in on it.

"He's innocent!" she says, her eyes frantic. "We have to get everyone out. NOW!"

Isabelle is right. The danger is far from over. Many students made it through the one open door on the other side of the atrium. Maybe even Xander. But hundreds more still press at the exit or gather around us for a better look, at Hogan—oh God, Hogan!

"It's going to be okay," I say to him, to myself, to Noah. To anyone that might be listening. "You're going to be okay."

I glance around the atrium knowing that the bomb could be hidden anywhere, could explode at any moment. Could kill every one of us. Hope and time are running out. Seeping through my fingers, like Hogan's blood.

And I just can't stop it.

HOGAN

My chest is on fire. My legs numb.
Oh my God—I've been shot!
The thudding in my ears slows.
Am I dying?

For the second time today, I ask myself that same question.
Only this time, I am shot. I am bleeding. I am injured. I don't
know how bad.

You look like hell, Hulkster.

It's Randy.

He is sitting beside me, glinting in and out of the shaft of
sunlight like he is only dust. He smiles. But this time, it isn't
mocking. He seems glad to see me.

Randy? My mouth doesn't move. Am I dying?

Randy shrugs. *It's up to you.*

I'm sorry, I say. I'm so sorry about everything.

I know. He nods slowly. *It was an accident. It wasn't your fault.*

And though the burning in my chest continues, the heavy weight has lifted.

He flickers.

What's it like where you are? I ask. Are you okay?

It's like a winning touchdown that lasts forever. He smiles and flickers again. *Don't worry about me, I'm good. We're good. And I'll be waiting for you, whenever it's time. But I'd say you got a few more plays to go, Hulkster. You're going to—*

"—be okay," Alice says next to me. Her voice pulls me like a lifeline. And my mind reaches for it, my heart holds onto it with whatever I've got left.

I look back. Randy is gone, but through the beam of sunlight I see the birds. His bird. And I see something else. A guy. Shimmying from a second-floor window across the wire that secures the big white bird to the wall. He's on the wire scrunching and stretching, inching along it like a caterpillar. Making his way to the center of the flock where a red ball dangles.

I grip Alice's hand.

ISABELLE

The police don't let Noah go, but they seem to ease up on him.

Hogan is sprawled on the floor. Alice is beside him, holding his hand. She has her other hand pressed tight against his chest. There's blood—a lot of blood. It's spilling through her fingers. Puddling on the floor. But I make myself kneel down beside them.

"Guys, we have to get out of here."

"He can't move until the paramedics come," Alice says. And I can tell she means that she won't either.

He's lost a lot of blood. How much is too much?

Hogan mumbles as he stares off, eyes glazed.

"Just relax," I say, but he lets go of Alice's hand and slowly points up at the Doves of Peace, where something among the large birds catches my eye. "Xander?"

It is. He has somehow made it across the wire and he's strad-dling one of the birds high overhead. A good thirty feet in the air.

What the hell is he doing?

The flying X is not shooting any more—maybe it's out of paint bullets—but it's buzzing him, diving and clipping at Xander's head. He ducks and swats at it, slipping sideways on the bird as he loses his grip. The sculpture sways dangerously.

"Careful!" I shout.

The plane buzzes by again. I may not know what Xander's up to, but whatever it is, clearly Maxwell is trying to stop him. Then I see it: a red shape among the birds. It's hanging on a long wire just out of Xander's reach. It's the Magneto helmet from the video.

The bomb!

But can Xander get to it? In time? And even if he does, does he know how to defuse it?

I look across the atrium. Hundreds of students cram the exit. All of them, all of us, right beneath a bomb that could go off any second. Could fire hundreds of bullets. In all directions. Could kill us all.

Alice and Hogan meet my eyes and we look back up at Xander Watt—the only one who can save us.

Xander pumps his legs, swinging the bird back and forth. The Tank, still around his neck, clatters against the wire. He's going to kill himself before he gets anywhere near that helmet. I worked on a dove back in grade 10 Art class. Randy King's. They are just fiberglass frames covered with papier-mâché, secured to the ceiling and walls with wire. Wire meant to bear the weight of one bird. Not a person. Especially not one swinging from it.

I expect each swing to be the last. The one where the sculp-ture splits, the wire snaps, or the bolts just rip right out of the wall. Total disaster—for Xander. For all of us.

But on the next pump, Xander springs off the bird and lunges for the helmet. The left cable of his bird snaps as he leaves and the bird drops, swooping towards the right wall. Even as the dove plunges, I hope it will pull up at that last second. But it rams the wall, hard, its head breaking into splinters, before it crashes to the floor.

Xander hangs from the helmet's wire, spinning high above the atrium like a circus performer while the drone attacks.

But this isn't a show. There's no net. And that isn't a helmet. It's a bomb.

Worst of all, time is running out.

"Forget the drone!" I yell up at him from where I kneel.

"Focus, Xander," Alice shouts. "You can do it!"

Ignoring the drone, Xander rolls upwards, and wraps his feet around the wire. Dangling by his legs, he starts yanking at the front of the helmet. He's tugging, tearing, trying to pull something from the eye sockets. Then, with one final heave, it comes free—

—and so does he.

The wire securing the helmet to the ceiling snaps and Xander drops. Thirty feet. Three seconds, if that, but it all happens in slo-mo:

His right arm windmilling—

his legs kicking as he tries to tread air—

the Tank floating just above him, strap slack as it falls—

and tucked like a football in the crook of his left arm: Magneto's helmet

red metal shining as it passes through the ray of light—

the bomb drops—

and Xander falls—

—just like the dove.

Alice throws herself over Hogan, covering their heads with her arm. But I just watch it all fall. Horrified. I wait for it to explode.

There is no blast. Just a sickening—CRACK!—as Xander hits.

He lies, not ten feet away, on the atrium floor beside the broken dove. His legs splayed. Head turned away. He doesn't

271

move. No one does. The Tank is shattered beside him. Its film unspools, exposing its brown guts. All of his pictures, his stupid pictures, dying in the light. He has that damn helmet still gripped in his arm. Through the ragged hole torn in its face falls a thin stream of ball bearings.

Click.

Click.

They hit the marble floor. Each one the sound of a life spared. Xander's right hand still holds whatever he ripped from the helmet. Wires. A digital display.

Click.

Click.

Click.

The small, silver balls glint in the light and then roll into darkness, as I watch the red numbers count down.

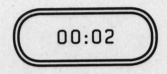
00:02

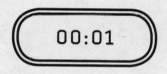

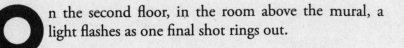On the second floor, in the room above the mural, a light flashes as one final shot rings out.

Then all is silent.

May 14, 2016

'On a rampage,' say peers

By Todd Ryder
Staff Writer

BIRCHTOWN—A 17-year-old student involved in yesterday's shooting at St. Francis Xavier High School has "always had anger issues," classmates said.

Multiple sources confirm this ex-linebacker was well known for his temper, arrests for drug use and theft, and antisocial behavior.

One 14-year-old student said she's "not surprised the cops shot him," while countless others stated that "the Hulk," as he is commonly known, was "naked and on a rampage" through the school only moments before the "police took him down as he attacked one of the high-needs kids."

One grade 9 student reported seeing four seniors fleeing him on the third floor as they escaped the boys' washroom, where he may have held them captive.

In interviews, students agreed that they thought the incident at the school was "just another X-Men

prank," an ongoing tradition this year at St. Francis Xavier. Whether "the Hulk" is the mastermind behind these X-Men stunts of false alarms, vandalism, and social disturbances remains to be seen. But parents, students, and administration all agree that it had escalated far beyond mere high school pranks.

"It's those damn video games," said one mother. Others blame heavy metal music, violent comics, and lack of funding for certain medications. Whatever the influence, one thing remains certain: the school community demands action.

"I don't care if he's under age. He's taken it to the next level," said one concerned parent. "It's time the justice system does the same. And if they don't, I will. Someone has got to teach this kid a lesson."

Speculations persist concerning the teenager's involvement in a previous altercation at the school in 2014 that resulted in the death of

277

his brother. Charges in that case were not laid.

Last night, masked paintballers vandalized the teen's home. His parents were unavailable for comment.

Regional Police also refused to comment on either the student's previous arrests or their investigation into this shooting.

Several students were admitted to hospital with injuries sustained during the attack. Two remain in critical condition, and one is confirmed dead.

ISABELLE

The school shuts down for a week—and so do I. After filling out police reports and interview after interview at the station, I got into my bed and stayed there. They'd interviewed me for hours. Separated us, so we'd keep our stories straight, I suppose. But it was only me and Alice. Noah doesn't speak. And Hogan and Xander—who knows if they will speak again?

I stay in bed—but I don't remember sleeping. I'm just replaying those scenes. That day. Those sixty minutes.

Was it only sixty minutes?

Images loop through my mind, like a slideshow of Xander's demented photos: Xander—sprawled on the atrium floor. Hogan's blood all over Alice's hands. Noah freaking out. Smoke. Chains. Ambulance lights. And all the while the alarm still ringing in my ears. At least, until . . . BANG! the gun explodes—and I wake again.

My parents let me be, at first. One day rolls into another. I don't eat or shower or care.

"Fresh air," my mother says, finally barging in and pulling open the curtains. Sunlight burns my eyes. "That's what you need." She moves to the clutter on my desk. Pins a ribbon back on my bulletin board. Starts picking up my pencils. Organizing. Obsessing. Fixing.

I don't speak. She'll never get it. Never get me.

My mother stops rearranging my pen caddy and instead sits on the bed beside me. She looks around at the mess that is my room and sighs.

I close my eyes—just waiting for her to tell me I'd feel better if I took a shower or cleaned my room.

"Do you want another Tylenol?" She rests the back of her hand against my forehead but there's no fever. "Why don't you call Brianne?" She pauses. "Her mom said she was in the office when it happened. She's probably upset."

"Who cares?" I mumble.

My mother looks around the room, unsure of what to do or say next. She never comes in here. I can tell she feels uncomfortable.

"Can I get you anything?" she asks, because she has no idea how to help. For a moment, I wonder if a real mom would know. If Teresa, my DREX mom, would know. My mother doesn't do well with this kind of nurturing—these kinds of needs.

"Juice . . . or toast or something . . ." She trails off into that awkward silence again.

If I wanted a ride or a new phone, if I needed money for school, she'd be all over that. But I don't even know what I need. So how can I ask for it?

"Is it . . . Darren?" she asks, her voice unusually gentle.

My eyes fill up. I look away.

"Did you guys have a fight?"

And then I see those pictures again—Darren and Bri. My Darren. My Bri. I feel sick.

"He cheated on me," I say, my voice low. "With Bri." I wasn't planning on thinking about it ever again. Least of all by telling her. The last thing I need is a pep talk about other fish, better friends, and new beginnings at Queen's—a place she still thinks I am going.

I close my eyes and rest my forearm across them, not wanting to see her disappointment in me as I add, ". . . And I didn't get into Queen's."

Hot tears seep out and roll back into my ears.

But instead of trying to cheer me up, or push me forward, instead of trying to pick me up and dust me off, instead of completely freaking out over my scars—which I just realize she has now seen—my mother does the one thing I never expected. She lies beside me. She wraps me in her arms. She kisses the top of my head, greasy hair and all. But she doesn't say a word.

We lie like that—and I cry. Like, snot-sobbing ugly-cry, until there's nothing left. And my mom cries too. But she never lets go. She just holds me tight, tight enough so that I can finally let go.

And that great big breath I've been holding for so long, years really—the one that makes my heart ache and shoulders tense, the one that makes my arms bleed—at last, it's released.

NOAH

RIIINNNG!
The lunch bell sings four seconds long.
    Kids get up and go.
And Mr. Dean and me
Sweep side to side.
                  All the way across.
And back.
                  Across.
And back.
Clearing crumbs and crusts
Spreading
                  quiet
                              clean
Like soft, flannel sheets.

Swish.

Swish.
Swish.

On the shiny square tiles.

It's nice.

ALICE

They let us back in after a week. The police wanted to be sure there were no other Maxwell surprises left behind. They say they got them all. But that doesn't help me. I still jump every time a locker slams. Panic in the crowds and stairwells and bathroom stalls. And even though I know they cleaned up the broken dove, and ball bearings, and . . . blood, I avoid the atrium altogether. A cold has settled in my gut, a trembling knot that ties me up and holds me hostage. Even now.

Fear.

It wakes me in the night. Hunts me in the day. I can't even write any more. It's as if my imagination has been poisoned— my greatest gift has become my worst enemy, conjuring threats and dangers everywhere. Every noise. Every person. Every story.

I envy Noah. Being back in school, back in his routine, is exactly what he needs. Noah lives in the moment, and probably doesn't even remember those ones I'll never forget.

Stories about Hogan spread far and wide and, of course, the media ran with them. Journalism is supposed to be based on fact—not rumors. But the reporters were too lazy, the sources too eager to gossip, and the readers too gullible. Some even blamed Mr. and Mrs. King for "what their son has done." That isn't journalism, at least not the kind of journalism Ms. Carter taught us. It's gossip. Sensationalism. Hysterical fiction.

Vandals struck the Kings' home with paint guns in retaliation. Worst of all, I heard it wasn't just kids. And by the time the official news release came from the police station—the one accusing Maxwell Steinberg and praising Hogan King as the hero who got us out, who alerted the principal, and who saved my brother—the King home had already been vandalized three times.

It shocks me how easily people believe the worst, how quick they are to point fingers and lay blame, and, sadly, how silent when at last they learn the truth.

Gran brought the Kings some baking that first week. Bite-sized support iced with butter cream. Typical Gran. I am glad she did, though. Because I wanted, I needed to hear how Hogan was doing. Not gossip or rumors. I needed to know he was going to be okay. His parents told Gran that he was out of the woods. The wound was healing and he'd need physio, but he'd be fine. I cried when she told me.

But Gran also baked for Ms. Steinberg. That, I still have a hard time with. I feel betrayed, in a way. I'm mad that she did it. Mad about a lot of things, I think, as we take the truck together to do Pet Therapy at the children's hospital.

"Why did you bake for Ms. Steinberg? This whole mess—it's all her son's fault," I finally say. "He tried to kill us, Gran."

Did she need reminding?

"Alice May Waters," Gran warns, and I know by her tone I'll not be getting any sympathy from her. "Don't tell me you've been swept up in their hate. You're a pitchfork away from joining the angry mob we saw on the news."

Once Maxwell was named in that police report, most people blamed his mom. Expert after expert and every neighbor interviewed on *The National*'s coverage was adamant that Maxwell's broken home life was the real problem. His mom's single parenting, her low income and lack of education, her drinking and boyfriends. They splattered all the dirt they could find on that family and, like those readers and viewers, I agreed.

"Ms. Steinberg needs understanding, now more than ever," Gran says. "No, she's not perfect. What family is?" She shakes her head. "I can just imagine what those 'experts' and 'neighbors' might have to say about ours!"

Gran is right. Like the saying goes: "Don't judge a book by the chapter you walk into." But I seem to do it all the time with people. I read a little bit of their lives and think I know them. Or worse yet, judge them entirely by the cover. We all do it, I guess. We buy into whatever story makes us feel better about our own. Make Maxwell a monster. Point fingers at the school system, or the medical system, or the family that failed him. Blame someone else. That way, we remain blameless.

But we're not. Not really. Because, the more I think about it, the more I realize that every one of us is a part of Maxwell's story. Even me.

"I know you're not a hateful person," Gran says, her voice softer now. "You're still scared. Understandably so."

She knows me so well. "I just want to crawl under my comforter and stay there for a while," I admit. "A long while."

"I know, love." Her hand reaches over and pats mine. "I felt the same after your grandfather passed. Couldn't imagine a life without him. Just the thought of trying to run the farm alone terrified me. And look at me now, driving the truck!"

I smile. Grampa always drove. All those years, I never even thought Gran could. She had a license, but she'd lost her nerve— so we took driver's ed together.

"If you face your fears, they lose their power," she explains.

"I know you're afraid, Alice. But that's why I make you go to school. And do your chores. And volunteer."

"But I've already got my mandatory volunteer hours," I argue. "Couldn't we have missed this, at least?"

"Mandatory volunteering? Now there's an oxymoron," Gran teases. "Besides, playing with the dogs is no work for you. And wee Ben would never forgive you for missing Pet Day."

I laugh. Ben sure wouldn't. His mom said the dog visits are the highlight of his week.

"Trust me," Gran says, "the best healing comes through helping others."

When we get to the hospital, I leave Gran and Noah with their dogs and head for the wing I'm visiting today. Buster squirms in my arms. For a puppy, he sure is a handful. But I know the patients enjoy the puppies the most.

As usual, the kids are waiting in the playroom for us. The regulars know our schedule, and as soon as we arrive, the room explodes in squeals and barks. And then I see him.

Hogan.

He sits on a small plastic chair across from the TV, holding a game controller in his left hand. A giant in Lilliput. He's playing against Ben, a regular here back for more chemo. But Ben bails on him and the game to chase after Buster. Hogan is wearing a muscle shirt and PJ bottoms, a sling over his right arm, and a growing smile. But it isn't directed at Buster. Or Ben. Or the kids playing and laughing. It's aimed in my direction. I think.

I look behind, just to be sure, but there's no one there.

And that chill I've carried these past days, that cold knot of fear in my gut, just loosens and melts away. Warmth spreads up my chest and across my cheeks. Hogan is okay. He's doing better.

Best of all, Hogan King is smiling. A great big grin.

And it's for me.

HOGAN

"**H**ey," I go.

"Hey." She sits in Ben's empty chair.

There's an awkward pause and we blurt out together, "How's your—?"

She smiles. "You first."

"How's Noah?"

"Good, now that he's back in his routine. Great, actually." She pauses. "What about you? How's your . . .?" She looks at my chest. "How's your gunshot?"

I snort. "Gunshot. I know, it sounds crazy, doesn't it?" I glance at the bandage. "The doctors hope I'll get full use of my arm when it heals, but I'll have a scar—a bullet wound." I smirk. "As if I wasn't badass before. I'm, like, a neck tattoo away from full-on thug."

"As if." She looks right at me.

"Yeah, well the newspapers—"

"Who cares what they said? You can't believe everything you read, you know."

I laugh. "One more reason to avoid reading."

Buster comes and flops on my feet. I bend down and pet him. His ears are like velvet flaps. He leans against me and licks my hand.

"He likes you," Alice says.

"I always wanted a dog but we could never have one because my brother has allergies."

Had allergies.

"Speaking of brothers," she pauses, "I never thanked you for saving Noah. If you hadn't been there . . ."

I shrug, unsure of what to say, because it wasn't even like I chose to save him. It just sorta happened.

"You're a hero, Hogan."

I look up at her. "A lot of people would disagree with you about that."

"Well . . ." her eyes glisten a bit, "fun fact . . . you're my hero." She blushes and looks away, but I hope it's not for long. Because maybe if she keeps looking at me like that, maybe I might believe it someday too.

Xander, he's the real hero. I think of him lying in the ICU up on the third floor. He still hasn't woken up. I wonder if he will. I wonder what will happen to him when he does.

I've been thinking about him a lot these past two weeks in here. There's not much else to do. Xander . . . he's not "the bad guy"—or "the good guy," really. He's both. Kind of like me, I guess. Neither of us wanted to hurt anyone. We just got carried along and caught up and then, suddenly, things went too far. And people got hurt.

Just like Randy.

I don't know what I saw that day in the atrium. Maybe it was Randy. Or maybe it was some adrenaline-shock-concussion-hallucination thing. All I do know is that since then, whenever

I think of Randy, I feel him with me. Beside me. Not pressing down on my chest like he used to. Come to think of it, that probably never was Randy. Anxiety, maybe? Or guilt? I can't explain it, really. All I know is that things feel different now.

Maybe it's just the bullet hole. Or the guy I saved. Or the way his sister looks at me.

But whatever it is, it's healing.

And it's good.

ISABELLE

The school had been reopened for a week and a half before I felt ready to go back. It was the last place I wanted to be, and I'd been avoiding Bri, Darren, everyone really. Even Alice. At least until Ms. Carter paired us up for peer editing of our final assignments for Writer's Craft.

Great. Just great. I drag myself over and sit across from her. So awkward. I don't know where to look or what to say. Red-faced, I shift in my seat.

"Ummm . . . we can just trade stories," Alice says, "and e-mail our feedback . . . if you want. We don't have to talk. I mean, I don't expect you to . . . just because we were . . ." She pauses and searches for the right words. "I get it. We're not real-real friends."

And I see how it looks to her. My avoidance since I came back to school. She's taking it personally.

"No. That's not it at all," I say. "Seeing you just reminds me of that whole horrible experience that I'd rather forget. No offense."

She looks at me skeptically.

"My meltdown . . . the picture . . ." I think of all the embarrassing things that came up that day.

Alice nods. "What happens in the men's room stays in the men's room."

She still doesn't get it. "You're a trigger," I say. "Seeing you brings it all back."

It makes sense, right? I saw something like that on an episode of *Dr. Phil.*

She frowns. "That's ridiculous!"

Ms. Carter looks over at us.

Alice leans in and whispers, "I see Noah every day. And Hogan every other day."

"Hogan?"

She blushes a bit. "He's out of the hospital now. Gran is helping him get his co-op hours at the kennel. So he can graduate."

"Are you . . . are you guys . . . dating?"

The pink spreads over her cheeks. Hogan and Alice? OMG. They totally are. Or will be.

"No," she says, her eyes betraying her hopes. "We're just friends."

"Real-real friends?" I tease.

And I realize that maybe we do have something more in common than the lockdown. Not that I want to, like, hang out with her or anything.

"Look, Isabelle. I know you're probably still freaked out by everything that happened. I know I sure am. But my Gran told me that you have to take it back." Her jaw is set in determination. "Take back the school. The atrium. We have to face the fear—whatever it is—or we'll be locked down forever."

And I realize that maybe this quirky girl with her oddball ways is right. Maybe she's on to something. And if someone like her can find the courage—maybe I can too.

"Girls," Ms. Carter interrupts, "you're supposed to be peer editing each other's stories."

"We are, miss," I lie without thinking, but then I realize it's the truth. I smile at Alice. "We, like, totally are."

ALICE

Up to my arms in soapy water, I lean over the sink full of dishes and peer out the kitchen window. I should be studying for my final exams, which start on Monday, but I can't concentrate. Hogan and Noah are out back trying to train the pups. I love watching them together. Hogan only needed a few more co-op hours to get his credit and, since we needed the help, Gran offered him a placement with our kennels. Even with his arm in a sling and a bullet wound to the chest he can still heft a huge bag of kibble from the truck and lug it, with the puppies and Noah trailing at his heels, over to the shed.

"It kind of defeats the purpose of having someone else with Noah if you're still gawking out the window after him. He's fine. They're fine," Gran teases as she picks up the tea towel to dry.

"I'm not. I just . . ." I busy myself with the pot-scrubber. "We'll miss having Hogan around when his hours are done. I mean, Noah will . . . and the dogs."

"Mmm-hmm," Gran says, knowingly.

Red-faced, I take a handful of bubbles and blow it at her. She laughs.

"Hogan!" she calls out the window. "Come in for a snack."

"Gran!" I scold her. "Don't—I just—"

"What, the boy can't come in for a rest and a glass of lemonade?" She puts down the tea towel and goes to the fridge. "Well, aren't you the taskmaster? And the poor boy fresh out of hospital with his arm still in a sling."

"All right, all right," I mutter, with a smirk. That Gran. She reads me like a book.

"I had a call," she says, serious now as she sets the lemonade and cookies on the table, "from Mrs. Goodwin yesterday. About your options for next year."

"I already told you, Gran, I'm not going to UBC." And I'm not. The more I picture it, me living on the other side of the country, the less desirable it seems. I said Noah needs me, but the truth is, I need him. And Gran, too.

"No," she continues, "not UBC, Carleton University, in town. They have a Creative Writing Program. It's not far, about forty-five minutes on the highway. You could live at home and—"

"And leave you and Noah to do all the work on the farm?" I say. It's a ridiculous idea.

Hogan and Noah come clattering in to the kitchen and sit at the table. Terrified that Gran will say something to embarrass me, I pick up a saucer, suddenly greatly interested in my scrubbing.

"Well, I won't be alone," Gran says, pouring Noah's drink. "Hogan will be here."

I stop and turn to look at them, oblivious to the soapy bubbles I'm dripping on the floor. "But your co-op here ends in a few weeks."

He grins. "And my job here starts after that."

"Really?" I say, my smile widening. I can't help it. "Really? You're working . . . here?"

"Well," Gran says, "only if I need the help. I mean, there's no sense in hiring on if you're going to be home just loafing about."

"Are you serious?" I say, my mind already skipping ahead. "But can we afford—?"

"Your grandfather took care of all that," she says. "Don't worry about the money."

My imagination races, looking for all the reasons it won't work. And finding none. "Then . . . yes! Yes!"

Hogan smiles at me.

"We have one condition, though," Gran says. "You have to dedicate your first novel to us—me, Noah, and Hogan."

And I throw my arms around her, suds and all.

ISABELLE

My shoes squeak on the hospital floor as I head for his room. This is the last place I thought I'd be—the last person I'd visit. To be honest, I'm not really sure why I came. I only know that I had to. That small voice inside me whispered—and, thanks to Alice, I listened.

He sits in a wheelchair at the table in his room playing Lego or something. He seems surprised to see me.

"Isabelle Parks." He announces me like some footman at a ball. But we are alone in the room.

"Xander Watt," I mimic. I sit across from him as he continues to sift through the bazillion gray pieces.

Fun.

"So . . ." I say, "how are you, like, feeling?" Stupid question.

He shrugs. Stupid answer.

He doesn't ask me why I'm here or what I want. Instead, he pushes a pile of gray Lego towards me and points at the diagram.

"Can you help me find this one?" His finger taps the drawing of some cube-shaped piece. It looks exactly like every other one. So, I start rummaging too. I never liked Lego. All the tiny bits. Hours building something just to take it apart. All that work—and nothing to show for it?

What's the point?

"What are you making?" I ask, like I care.

"Lego Death Star," he says, like it matters.

We sift in silence for a few minutes and then he says, in his oddball way, "My dad left me when I was nine."

I focus on the pieces, unsure of what exactly I should say to that.

"We were supposed to finish this together." After a few moments he continues. "But I've decided to do it myself. Maybe I don't need him after all."

I don't reply. But I don't really think he expects me to.

After a pause, I clear my throat and mimic his detached tone. "My birth mother left me in a box on the roadside."

A fact. One I've never told anyone. Still, it's just a fact. That's all. Just information. It's not a definition of who I am. Unless I let it be.

"Are you retconning too?" He looks up at me, suddenly interested.

"What?" I've no idea what he's talking about.

"Retroactive Continuity? It is when comic book writers change or rearrange a character's early life."

Oh, comics. Yay.

He keeps talking. "I know that changing up a backstory seems illogical and wrong because, well, the facts are true. What happened, happened. But sometimes it's not about the facts, it's about seeing the character's past in a new light—to make the story ahead even better."

I pull out my new iPhone to check the time. I should probably go.

"So, I have decided to retcon." He picks up a piece, examines it, and tosses it back in the box. Picks up another. "The stuff with Max. Maybe even all the way back to when Dad left."

And I realize that he's not still talking about his dumb comics. "Are you talking about yourself? Like, revising your life?"

Is that even possible?

I notice it then, the cube-shaped piece. I pluck it out of the box and hold it up. "Is this it?" I can't believe I found it—in all that gray mess. I'm amazed I found the key piece.

"If you could retcon, what would you change?" he asks.

"I'd go back to China," I say, without thinking. And suddenly, it all becomes clear. China. "I think I need to see where I came from before I can know where I'm going next."

The wish rings true somewhere deep inside me, like the surfacing of a long-forgotten secret.

"Who knows?" I add. "I might even take a year or two and volunteer in the orphanage or something."

He nods.

Then, remembering why I came, I pick up the camera hanging around my neck. Swiping my thumb over the switch, I turn it on as I raise it and look through the viewfinder. His shocked face fills the frame.

"Say CHEE-eese," I say, in my Yearbook Editor way.

He doesn't, in his Xander way.

Click.

If that didn't totally freak him out, now he gets even more awkward when I pull my seat over beside his wheelchair. His face gets all red. I take the strap off my neck and flip the camera around to show him the display.

"See? You can edit right on the camera." I press a few buttons and change the look. "Crop. Filters. Adjust the light. Or you can shoot black-and-white, if that's still your thing."

I hold it out. He looks at it, at me, back at the camera.

"I figured," I explain, "since your Tank got wrecked . . ."

He blinks. Repeatedly. He doesn't get it.

"My parents bought me a better one for graduation," I say. It surprised me, especially when Dad said it was Mom's idea—that she wanted to get me something special to help me follow my heart. That she knew how much I loved photography.

Maybe she knows me better than I thought.

"Anyway," I put it in his hands, "I don't need this, so it's yours. If you want it."

Xander slowly lifts the camera. Looks through the viewfinder. Tests the zoom.

I smile. "Hey, here's something your Tank couldn't do. Press this." I push the timer button. "Hold it about here." He does as instructed, holding it at arm's length with the lens facing down at us side by side.

3 . . .

2 . . .

1 . . .

Click.

Xander turns it around to see the display. A black-and-white shot of us. Optimal selfie angle, of course. My hair is perfect. My pose, cute. My smile, wide. But I hardly notice any of that. All I see is the look on Xander's face. The wonder in his eyes. The small grin tugging at the corner of his mouth.

He looks like a kid at Christmas.

XANDER

June 10, 2016
Dear Max,

It's been nearly a month since the lockdown. Four weeks since I've seen you. Four weeks that I've been stuck in this hospital waiting to see if my legs will work again. I have to use a wheelchair, just like Professor Xavier (it is not half as awesome as it sounds). But the doctor says I have an 80 percent chance of full recovery. He says that the body has amazing regenerative powers. (All this time, I had a superpower and didn't know it!)

I asked Mrs. O'Neill if everything broken might eventually heal, like a bone. She said that anything is possible. Actually, it was her idea to write you. She thought it might help.

I won't be going back to school this year. I gave the police all my logs and photos of our missions. And you know how good I am at remembering all the details. They know everything now. I know I vowed to you that I'd keep our X-Men Missions secret, but I can't keep that promise any more. I am sorry, Max.

What you did was wrong. And even if I never did anything but hold the camera or buy the stuff, what I did—not telling anyone, not listening to that little voice inside me that said we shouldn't—I get it now, that was wrong too.

Lately, I've been thinking about you and me and Mrs. O'Neill's Friendship Checklist. Yes, we had common interests, but the more I think about it, you were usually laughing at me, not with me. You often lied to me about your real plans and used me to get stuff. I thought we were friends, probably because you were the only one I ever had. But after doing a Social Autopsy, I must conclude, Max, that you did not see me as a friend.

Realizing this made me feel hurt and frustrated and just plain stupid. But Mrs. O'Neill helped me see what I had not noticed: I was always a good friend to you. I admired you. I helped you. I shared with you (remember my jet that I never got back?). I even gave you my dad's comics because I knew it would make you happy. I liked hanging out with you, Max. We had some good times. I'll miss that.

You taught me a lot of stuff, too, mainly about Marvel. Now, I love Marvel mutants. I totally relate to them. No, I cannot shoot laser beams from my eyes or adamantium claws from my knuckles—though that would be cool! I can't manipulate the weather, fire, or ice, or control minds or metal. But I know what it feels like to be different.

I think we both know what that's like.

I noticed something else, Max. In all the Marvel comics, the mutants start out hating what makes them different. But as they evolve they realize what it takes to raise a storm, read a mind, or even take a stand when no one else will.

Courage.

It takes courage to risk being different—but I think it's worth it. It's so worth it. Because what makes us different is what makes us powerful. And what we choose to do with that power can make us heroes.

And I choose to be a hero, Max.

I'm glad we met. Despite the ending, I'm still glad our stories mixed like a crossover series. Remember when you first told me about crossovers? I hated the idea of characters from one comic appearing in another. The Avengers should not be in a battle with the X-Men. Characters should stay in their own worlds where they belong. (Honestly, I don't even like it when my foods touch.) But then you showed me the A vs. X series . . . and I loved it! Almost as much as my Star Wars comics. You were right. It's good to mix things up sometimes. I think that if a character gets too comfortable the story gets predictable and boring. Other characters bring tension and conflict, problems and drama, lots of drama—but like Ms. Carter and Stan THE MAN Lee say, that's the key to a great story.

Maybe it's also the key to a great life.

I'm not sure when I'll be able to deliver your letter. I've seen the newspapers. I've read the horrible things the press is saying about you and your home life. But even if no one else cared about you—I did.

You mattered to me, Max. And I just wanted to let you know.

Your friend,
Xander

304

ACKNOWLEDGMENTS

The characters in this novel are fictional, but it still took a village to raise them. I wanted Izzy, Hogan, Alice, Xander, Noah, and Max to be relatable, recognizable, as real as possible, and that meant research. Lots of research. I am so thankful to my friends and colleagues who were key resources in developing each of these characters.

Thanks especially to:

—my kids, Liam and Marion. Liam, thanks for teaching me all about comics, even if you won't let me touch them. Marion, thanks for inspiring me with your amazing photography, and for your great shot, used in the last chapter. You guys are MARVELous. (See what I did there?)

—the fabulous gang at the 2014 Carver-Stinson Seaside Writing Workshop, who first met the novel's characters and gave me the courage to keep going. Thanks to Jocelyne Stone, Gwynn Scheltema, Shannon McFerran, Miriam Koerner, Joyce Major, and

Peter Carver, and a special thanks to Kathy Stinson for the insights and feedback in our one-on-one session. I came away from that week with great memories, new friends, fresh ideas, renewed confidence, and a newfound obsession with knitted socks.

—Constable Sean Carroll of the Ottawa Police Service, and Sandra Lemieux of the Children's Aid Society of Ottawa, for taking the time to answer my many questions about procedures and resources. Thanks for all you both do to keep our kids safe. You guys are amazing!

—my agent, Marie Campbell, who raises the bar, coaches me over it, and cheers me on. Without you, I'd still be wishing from the sidelines.

—Lynne Missen and her editorial team. Lynne, thanks for all the ways you helped me find these characters' voices. Thanks especially for believing in mine.

—Vikki VanSickle, for your enthusiasm, encouragement, and especially for helping me become a tweet-gramming fool. Thanks to you, I've found a whole new platform to promote my work and embarrass my kids.

—my parents, Peggy and Alan, and my husband, Tony, who always say they want to read my first draft (even if they don't) and always say it's good (even if it isn't). I would never have started writing without your encouragement. And would never have finished it without your mojitos.

And a special thanks to the awesome staff and students at All Saints High School, who inspire me daily. I am honored to share in your stories and grateful for the many ways you enrich mine. In particular, I'd like to thank:

—the All Saints grade 12 Photography class: Lina Akkawi, Savannah Atout, Jessica Box, Max G., Sydney Hill, Emily Hobson, Samuel Inkoom, Ashley Irwin, Jessica Jonas, Justin Kaluski, Kristen Langdon, Kathleen Lebel, Nicholas Lypps, Peter M., Morgan O., Janelle Rowsell, Trisha Santos, Bianca Texeira, Jacob Tynski, Justin Winters, Nathan Yee, and their fabulous teacher, Graham Mastersmith. Thank you for taking on Xander's photos as a class assignment and for showing us the world through his lens.

—Carolyn Dyer and Jennifer Percival, for your photography support.

—Erin Connolly, for being a fabulous mad scientist and prank imagineer.

—Jenn Scrim and your wonderful group of Educational Assistants in the High Needs Room, whose resources and recommendations helped me come to know Noah's experience and perspective.

—Cheryl Orzel, Danielle Baillie, and Sydney Dowd, for sharing your amazing insights and profound experiences on DREX trips.

—Wendy MacPhee, Amy Talarico, and Donelda Pleau, for your knowledge, wisdom, and wonderful empathy both inside and outside the Resource Room.

—our amazing Student Services and Administration teams, who patiently answered my countless bizarre questions that began with, "Hypothetically speaking, if a student . . ."

—every hero that I have journeyed with in my grade 12 Writer's Craft classes. I'm so glad our stories crossed, even if it was just for one semester. I hope your adventures continue to be epic.

Thanks to you all for being in my village!

Caroline Pignat is the award-winning author of seven YA novels. She is a two-time winner of the Governor General's Award (*The Gospel Truth* in 2015 and *Greener Grass* in 2009). *Unspeakable*, a Red Maple Honour Book, was also shortlisted for the 2015 CLA Young Adult Book Award and the Geoffrey Bilson Award for Historical Fiction for Young People. A high school teacher, she lives in Ottawa with her family. Visit her at www.carolinepignat.com.